THE GILDED DAYS

MIA KENT

The Gilded Days

By Mia Kent

Be the first to know about new releases! Sign up for my newsletter here. Your information will never be shared.

CHAPTER 1

Summer 1957

Henry Turner walked quickly through the streets of Dolphin Bay, his eyes on the dusky purple sky. It was quiet at this time of the evening, when most of the businesses that lined the town's main road had closed their shutters and the only sound drifting to him on the wind was the conversation coming from Stetson's Pharmacy, where old man Stetson kept his soda fountain counter open until nine o'clock for the younger crowd.

Henry resisted the urge to stop in as he passed by; Stetson's had the best homemade cherry soda in all of Maine, and Henry and Penny had spent many evenings sitting in side-by-side chairs at the counter, laughing and chatting about their day. And making plans for the future, of course, the way they'd been doing since they were kids and the first blush of romance had risen between them, somewhere in between the scraped knees and the games of tag on the island's golden-sand beaches.

Their friends may have teased them—the girls giggling behind cupped hands and the boys wiggling their eyebrows in Henry's direction every chance they got—but he and Penny didn't care. They were in love. Henry figured that some people were just meant to be together, and for better or for worse, Penny was his girl. Now and forever.

His breath sharpened at that last thought, and his fingers automatically dipped into the pocket of his pants, as they'd been doing every five seconds since he left the inn to meet Penny at their usual spot. He was terrified of losing the ring he'd scrimped and saved for nearly a year to purchase; every dollar he made stocking shelves at Prantle's Grocers, every tip he pocketed from carrying guests' luggage up the stairs at the inn his family had been running for two generations, heck, every coin he scraped out of the sand left behind when the tourists departed for the day—all of it went toward that ring.

The sparkling sapphire reminded him of Penny's ocean-blue eyes, and the thin gold band would be the perfect fit for her delicate fingers. After so many years of dreaming and planning, of talking about the future they had always envisioned, he was finally about to make it happen. And he couldn't think of a better time to pop the question than tonight, the day after he and Penny had graduated from the island's small high school. They were about to take on adulthood head-on, and they would do it together.

The chatter floating out from Stetson's was soon replaced by the rustling dune grass and the gentle crashing of the waves against the shore as Henry left the island's main drag behind and headed to the spot that he and Penny had claimed as their own. It wasn't really theirs, of course, but the weathered wooden bench at the farthest end of the island's boardwalk was almost always empty; even during the height of the summer season, the island's residents and tourists alike preferred to mill around the souvenir stalls or buy ten-cent ice cream cones or watch one of the live shows taking place on the boardwalk's small, makeshift stage.

But not Henry. Even as a boy, he felt the ocean calling to him somewhere deep in his soul, felt its tug like gravity any time he neared the island's stunning blue-gray waters. Let the tourists come, with their bright umbrellas and their shouting children and their pieces of bread they delighted in tossing to the island's ever-present seagulls. As long as they left him and Penny this little corner of the world, this little slice of paradise, he was happy.

The island grew wilder the farther he got from town, and he passed dune grass as high as his waist and wild native plants bursting with coral and yellow flowers before he caught sight of the boardwalk, glowing carnival colors in the distance. When his family had first settled on the island, many years before Henry was born, the boardwalk was nothing more than a row of planks stretching out into the water. In recent years, the mayor had decided to increase Dolphin Bay's appeal to tourists by creating a boardwalk that was reminiscent of Coney Island or some of the hot spots on the Jersey Shore.

Even though Henry would have preferred that the island remain pristine and secluded, he had to admit that the Ferris wheel, a recent addition, was worthwhile. He and Penny loved to catch the last ride, late into the evening when most of the tourists had gone back to their rooms and the air was heavy with humidity and the sweet scent of flowers and saltwater.

They would sit in their cart, as close as they dared, and gaze up at the blanket of stars while imagining what the future would be like. Both he and Penny wanted to travel, to see the world beyond the island's rocky coastline and windswept shores, but they would return to beautiful Dolphin Bay to settle down and raise their family. Two boys, two girls, and a Labrador.

A smile lingered at the corners of Henry's lips as he climbed the sandy boardwalk steps and wove through the few people who lingered there this evening: a young couple holding hands and gazing out at the darkening sky, a group of younger teenagers Henry knew from school skipping stones into the water. He waved as he passed them, and they acknowledged him with cheerful salutes and calls of "G'night, Henry!" before returning to their game. On any other night he may have joined them, staying up until the moon danced across the waves and the seagulls' cries had quieted, but not tonight.

Tonight, he had more important things to do.

She was already waiting for him on their bench, the last rays of the setting sun casting orange highlights in her light hair and softly illuminating her impossibly beautiful face. The crashing waves muffled his footsteps, so she remained unaware of his presence as she stared out over the dark water, her hair blowing around her cheeks, her eyes closed. She looked so peaceful that he didn't want to disturb her, but when he set his foot on a creaky plank she gave a little start, blinking rapidly as if pulling herself from a trance, before giving him that smile that had made him go weak in the knees since they were kids.

"Hi." She patted the bench and shifted aside to make room for him.

He kissed her gently on the cheek and dropped onto the bench beside her, his fingers automatically reaching for his pocket again before he stopped himself, clenching them into fists at his sides instead. Penny was sharp—much sharper than Henry, and he had no problems admitting it—so he didn't want to clue her in on what was happening. Sure, they'd talked about marriage plenty of times, but now... now, it was real. And he desperately wanted the proposal to be a surprise.

"Hi." Henry took her hand in his and squeezed it as his heart suddenly began pounding way too fast. He could feel beads of nervous sweat springing up on his brow, and he turned his head away as discreetly as he could before swiping them away with a quick flick of his hand.

"Last night was fun, wasn't it?" Penny nestled against him and rested her head on his shoulder, her long hair falling into his lap. "I thought I'd be sad about finishing high school, but... I don't know. I'm excited about what's going to come, I guess. I'll miss everyone, though."

"Me too," Henry murmured into the top of her head, thinking of the friends who would soon be making their way into the world. They had grown up together, the island their playground and the sea the setting to every important moment in their lives, but now, many of them would be headed off to college, or jobs on the mainland, or to try their luck in a bigger city. Henry would miss them, but he wouldn't envy them in the least. The island was his home, the very blood running through his veins—he knew it, and someday they would too.

He breathed a small, inaudible sigh of relief, grateful once more that he and Penny were on the same page.

They sat in silence for a long time, the way they always did, the ebb and flow of the ocean waves mirroring their breathing, which was in sync as they gazed out at the open water. The hazy outline of the mainland was visible in the rising glow of the moon, and the ferry that shuttled residents and visitors to and from the island was chugging into the harbor to deliver its last fares of the night.

Although he tried to relax, the sapphire ring felt like it was burning a hole in Henry's pocket, and he inadvertently held his breath as he mentally rehearsed the speech he had been preparing for so long. He had planned to wait until later in the evening to deliver it, when the stars were fully visible and twinkling down on them like sentinels, but he realized he couldn't wait one more moment to tell her all the things he wanted her to hear. How she was a dream he never wanted to wake from. How he had known she was his from the moment he laid eyes on her, so many years ago. How he wanted to get married right away, because he couldn't wait one more second for their future to begin.

He took a deep breath, ran a trembling hand through his hair, and shifted on the bench, preparing to drop to one knee on the damp, salt-stained boardwalk.

"I have news."

Penny's voice was like a gunshot in the stillness, and he reared back inadvertently, the ring rattling in his pocket. He quickly pressed his hand against it and tried to catch his breath.

"You okay?" Penny was giving him an odd look, and he hurriedly arranged his features into a smile.

"Never better." He crossed one leg over the other nonchalantly, though by now his heart was pounding so hard he was beginning to feel slightly off-kilter. "You were saying you had news?"

"I do." Penny grinned at him, her eyes shining

with excitement. She took a deep breath, then said, "I got into journalism school. It's one of the most prestigious programs in the country, and they made it co-educational this year. I'll be the first woman in the program." She gripped his hand tightly, her nails digging into his skin, though she seemed not to notice. "And Henry, you'll never guess where it is." She gave a dramatic pause while she looked at him with an expectant expression. "Go on, guess."

She didn't seem to realize that Henry was staring at her in horror, or that he had stopped breathing, or that his face had suddenly lost every last speck of color. His throat felt like it was closing in as he watched her face blankly, his mind working rapidly behind the scenes as he tried without success to process what she was telling him. Journalism school? Penny had never mentioned a word to him about applying to college. He scoured every corner of his mind, trying to recall even a hint of a conversation that he had somehow missed, but there was nothing.

Nothing at all.

By now, Penny had grown tired of waiting. "New York City!" she squealed, her voice so high-pitched that the other couple on the boardwalk glanced their way. "Oh, Henry, it's going to be just like we imagined, just like we've been talking about all these years. We're going to see the world together, and what better place to start than the most exciting city on earth?"

She was talking faster now, color rising to her cheeks as she began imagining the shows they would see, the restaurants they would visit, the museums they would tour—all the things that a quiet life on Dolphin Bay couldn't provide. The more she talked, the more Henry's lungs constricted, until his breaths were coming out in short, strangled gasps. None of this—*none* of it—was in their plans.

"Henry, what's wrong?"

He hadn't even realized Penny had stopped talking until she had taken his hand and given it a little shake. Her lips were pursed, her brows furrowed in concern. "I know I've sprung this on you and didn't tell you I was applying to school or anything, but..." She trailed off, chewing her bottom lip anxiously. "First of all, I didn't think I was going to get in, and I thought... well, I thought you'd be a little more excited. Isn't this the life we've always talked about? You and me, seeing the world together?"

Yes, yes it was. But at the end of the day, they were supposed to come back to the island. Henry's father would be retiring in the not so distant future, and as the only child, he would take over the running of the inn. It was the life that was destined for him, the life that he desperately wanted.

Did he want to visit New York City? Sure, as much as the next guy. And Rome and Tahiti and Hawaii and all those other places where tourists flocked to and glossy brochures beckoned from, but at the end of the day—at the end of his life—he wanted to be sitting on the inn's wraparound porch with a glass of lemonade in one hand and Penny's hand in the other, watching their children, their grandchildren, their great-grandchildren build sand-castles and dance in and out of the waves rolling to shore. It wasn't just something he wanted—it was something he *needed*.

And exactly zero journalists made Dolphin Bay their home. The island didn't have anything even *resembling* a newspaper, for crying out loud.

"Henry? Say something, will you?" Penny's voice was edged with concern as she studied his face anxiously. He opened his mouth to reply, to tell her all the things he was thinking, but he could only gape at her instead, his mouth opening and closing like a beached fish.

"Henry?" Now her tone was filled with full-on panic. "You will come to New York with me, won't you? I know it's not the island, but you and I... we were made for each other. We could be happy anywhere, couldn't we? It's just..."

She was wringing her hands in her lap, her knuckles going white from the effort. "You know how much I love to write, and there are opportunities opening up all over the world for women now. I want to make something of my life, you know? I still want it all—the house, the babies, the white-picket fence, the Labrador"—she nudged him playfully —"but I need to use my brain, too."

She let her voice trail off, and her gaze returned to the dark water. The wind had picked up, and tendrils of hair were whipping around her face, but she didn't make a move to swipe them away.

When she met his gaze again, her eyes were shining with tears. "We could be happy anywhere, couldn't we?" she repeated, though this time her words were so small that they were nearly carried away on the wind.

Henry stared at her for a long time, his eyes seeking out every line of her face, every freckle on her nose, every wisp of blonde hair twirling around her head. He was committing them to memory, to an eternity of what-ifs and if-onlys and what-might-have-beens.

"Of course we could," he finally said, wrapping his arm around her shoulders and pulling her close to him. And though they remained like that for hours, staring out over the endless sea as the precious moments of their youth—of their inno-cence—ticked away, Henry never once dipped his hand into his pocket, never once felt the ring's cold, smooth reassurance that the future was laid out before them like a red carpet, ready for them to walk together.

CHAPTER 2

"*N*o. I don't want it."

Tana Martin closed her eyes wearily and massaged her temples with her fingertips, trying to ward off the migraine that had been threatening to make an appearance all day. "Why not?" she asked for the umpteenth time, doing her best to give her ornery old great-uncle a patient smile that was beginning to make her cheeks hurt. This final meeting with the contractor Tana hired to make the necessary repairs and updates to the inn was not going as smoothly as she had planned, mainly because of Uncle Henry's unwillingness to see anything change.

"Because it's always been done that way, that's why." Henry tried crossing his arms, then seemed to remember that his left one was still mostly immobile due to his recent stroke. Instead, he settled on fixing Tana with a glare that would have sent most people running for the hills.

But right now, Tana was undeterred—her job was to oversee the renovations to the Inn at Dolphin Bay, her great-uncle's beloved business that had fallen into disrepair. Any grouchiness and petulant-child behavior her uncle could throw her way—and he seemed to be trying his best to do it at least once a minute—wouldn't make her back down.

"Uncle Henry, that's not a good reason." Tana's voice was tight with annoyance as Luke, the contractor she had hired after interviewing several candidates, looked on in bemusement. So far during this walk-through of the inn, he was watching the two of them like he was at a tennis match, his head swiveling from Tana to Henry and back again as they argued over everything from the color of the windowsills to the current disagreement: whether each of the inn's guest rooms should have a private bathroom.

"Look," she said, more gently this time, trying her best to make the old man see reason. "I know these changes are hard for you, Uncle Henry, but right now, we need to look at the bigger picture: what's best for the inn. Only six of the ten rooms for rent have private bathrooms, and you know as well as I do that it's always been a sticking point for the guests. Those rooms are always the last to rent, and as far back as I can remember, the guests staying in them have requested to move to a different room as soon as possible. These days, people want privacy. It isn't the 1950s anymore."

What made her say that last line, Tana didn't know, but Uncle Henry's reaction was visceral—he reared back from her, his face contorted as though the mention of those days caused him actual pain.

Which, she reminded herself, it probably did. Although Tana's uncle had asked for help locating the mysterious Penny nearly a month ago, each time she tried to broach the subject with him since then, he shut down. How Tana was supposed to find her uncle's long-lost love with nothing but a first name to go on was beyond her, but that was a problem for another time.

"Luke." She turned to the contractor with a look of desperation, hoping he would help Henry see reason. "You're the expert here—tell me, would you recommend adding a bathroom to the rooms that don't have one?"

"Absolutely." Luke ignored Uncle Henry's grunt of annoyance, focusing on Tana instead. "It's pretty much a must these days if you want the inn to be fully booked. Like you said, people like separation.

They don't want to mingle with strangers during their vacations."

He shrugged and shot Henry a sympathetic look. "If you ask me, it's nice to meet new people, but I don't think that's the norm anymore. Take my ex-wife, for instance. She flat-out refused to book a stay at this beautiful beachfront hotel down in Florida for our honeymoon because the patios didn't have a wall separating them." He snorted. "She said she didn't want anyone staring at her while she ate her French toast in the morning."

"See?" Tana crossed her arms over her chest and stared Uncle Henry squarely in the eye.

He glared right back at her for several long moments while Luke gazed out the window, pretending to be admiring the room's sweeping ocean views, but she could tell by the tension in his shoulders and the tightness of his jaw that he was feeling uncomfortable. Not that Tana could blame him—she and Uncle Henry had been squabbling in the contractor's presence all morning.

"Fine." The old man finally looked away, leaning heavily on his cane as he did his best to hobble around the inn on his one good leg. "I guess you're the boss now, so what's the point in me even giving my opinion? It's not like I've been running the place for the past sixty years."

Running it into the ground, Tana thought as her uncle stomped away, and then immediately felt ashamed of herself. For five of those six decades, the inn had been pristine and an immensely popular vacation destination; only in the last ten years, after her uncle had fallen into some financial trouble, had things begun to deteriorate. But that would soon be a problem of the past. Henry had agreed to let his great-niece take charge of rehabbing the inn from top to bottom, and she had thrown herself into the job wholeheartedly. Not only because she wanted the beloved inn from her childhood to rise from the ashes, but also because it provided a welcome distraction from her divorce-in-progress.

Which reminded her... Tana caught sight of the clock on the wall and winced. In a few hours she would be catching a flight to Los Angeles to begin the dreaded task of packing up the house she and her soon-to-be ex-husband Derek used to share, and the prospect of stepping back into the place that held so many memories of happier times made her stomach clench with panic.

She'd done her best over the past few weeks to push Derek—and the infidelity that had destroyed their marriage of over twenty years—out of her mind, but his decision to dump her for a young, stunningly gorgeous Italian actress named Lucia made for the kind of tabloid fodder that Tana's former social circle couldn't get enough of. She could imagine the expressions of glee on her friends' faces as they spouted fake sympathy for poor Tana's predicament over bottomless champagne and dressing-less salads at whatever Hollywood hotspot they'd chosen for their weekly luncheon. Not one of them had thought to call her or offer any type of support in the aftermath of Derek's betrayal, other than Selene, her neighbor and the closest thing she had to a true friend in Los Angeles.

"So is that okay? Ma'am?" Tana gave a start as she realized that Luke had been trying to get her attention, and she quickly pulled her thoughts away from Derek and the life she was leaving behind and refocused on the task at hand.

"I'm sorry, my mind drifted away for a moment there. I guess you could say I'm a little overwhelmed." Tana gave him a small smile. "You were saying?"

"No problem." Luke grinned at her, and not for the first time, she noticed how handsome he was. She wondered if he had ever been introduced to Daphne, her childhood friend from the island she had recently reconnected with. "I was just saying that I'll spend the rest of the day getting my ducks in a row, placing calls to the subcontractors and developing a renovation timeline, and then I'll be on your doorstep bright and early tomorrow morning. Does that work for you folks?"

"Absolutely," Tana said hurriedly, noticing out of the corner of her eye that Uncle Henry was opening his mouth, presumably to find something to argue about. "This might be too much to hope for, but if we can be up and running, at least partially, by the end of summer, I'll be thrilled."

"I'll do everything I can to make that happen."

Luke followed Tana back to the inn's front desk —Uncle Henry stomped off to his first-floor room, leaning heavily on his cane—and began laying out a row of paperwork for her to sign. While she read through the pages, he gazed out the floor-to-ceiling windows that lined the inn's parlor, admiring the stunning view of the blue-gray waters of the Atlantic and the red-and-white lighthouse that overlooked the Dolphin Bay harbor.

"This place is really something," he said when Tana handed the papers back to him and tucked the pen behind her ear. "I'm not sure I've ever seen a view like this from a hotel in my life. To tell you the truth, I'm honored to have the opportunity to make this beautiful inn shine again." He grinned at her. "Promise you'll invite me to the grand reopening celebration?"

"You'll be the first name on the list," Tana assured him, holding out her hand for him to shake. Then she watched as he left the inn, jogging down the porch steps and the cobblestone sidewalk before sliding into the driver's seat of his golf cart and heading back into town.

Tana was glad to be hiring a local contractor for the job—she'd interviewed several companies on the mainland, but Luke had grown up on the island and knew just how special the inn was to the people who lived here, along with the families who had made it their vacation destination every summer. And his idea of a grand reopening celebration couldn't be more perfect—although the thought of having to convince Uncle Henry to co-host a party with her elicited a groan of frustration as Tana slumped into the chair behind the desk, suddenly feeling exhausted.

"Hello! Anyone home?" Edie, the older woman who owned the antique shop just down the road from the inn, popped her head in the front door and waved to Tana. Then she looked past her with a frown and shook her head. "Don't tell me—that old bag of bones is holed up in his room again, sulking. Am I right, or am I right?"

"You're right," Tana said, trying to suppress a giggle. Edie was probably her reclusive uncle's only true friend in this world, and according to Daphne, the two of them were secretly in love. Edie's son Reed liked to disagree vehemently every time the subject came up, but even he had to admit that his mother had an obvious soft spot for Henry, and he for her.

And speaking of soft spots… These days, even the thought of Reed brought color to Tana's cheeks. Her attraction to him had started almost immediately upon meeting him, but they had yet to progress to anything beyond friends. Tana had been with Derek since she was in college, and the idea of putting herself out there again made her feel vaguely nauseous. She had no idea even *how* to date. What was she supposed to wear? Or do? Or say?

Luckily, Reed had never even hinted at the possibility of taking things to the next level, and right now, Tana was totally fine with that. The swift and painful demise of her marriage still occupied a good portion of her thoughts, although Tana was hoping that cleaning out the house and preparing it for sale would go a long way toward helping her find closure. Then, she would leave California behind for good—Derek, broken heart, and all.

"What's he mad about this time?" Edie said, interrupting Tana's thoughts. The older woman was peering at Uncle Henry's closed bedroom door with her hands on her hips, though her eyes were twinkling merrily. "Did you tell him you were thinking about changing the brand of toilet paper he uses in the guest bathrooms? I can imagine the kind of fit he'd pitch about *that*."

"He's mad about anything and everything," Tana said, removing the pen from behind her ear and twirling it around in her fingers. "But you know what I think?" She leaned toward Edie and lowered her voice confidentially. "I think he's really just upset about Penny, and the prospect of me finding her after all these years. He just can't—or won't—put those feelings into words."

"Ah, Penny." Edie's smile faltered, and she tucked a strand of silver hair behind her ears as she gazed once more over Tana's shoulder toward the bedroom door. "Well, I hope you find her... and I hope that when you do, Henry finds what he's looking for."

She tugged her ruby-red shawl around her shoulders and took a step toward the front door. "I have to be going now, but I wanted to wish you good luck with your time in California. Stop by the shop when you get back to the island and we'll have a cup of tea together."

"That sounds lovely," Tana said, watching as the older woman turned and walked out the inn's front door, though she was missing the usual spring in her step. She barely had time to reflect on Edie's sudden change in mood, however, because her phone chose that moment to begin buzzing in her pocket. Smiling when she saw her daughter Emery's name on the caller ID, Tana immediately answered the call.

"Mom, how are you doing?"

Emery, currently studying fashion design in New York City, had chosen to stay for the summer semester, and Tana missed her deeply. Although she had to admit that it was a good thing her daughter hadn't been in Los Angeles to witness the implosion of her parents' marriage, the brutal end of what had once been a fairy-tale love story.

Or so Tana had thought.

"Great," Tana said, doing her best to inject a note of cheeriness into her tone. She glanced at the clock hanging above the front desk, which seemed to be moving at warp speed all day, though Tana would have given anything for it to come to a complete standstill.

"How are you *really* doing?" Emery's voice was soft, and Tana once again felt grateful that she and Derek had managed to raise such a caring, kind, thoughtful girl. "I know you're dreading going back home, Mom. Are you sure you don't want me to come with you? If we both pack up the house, it'll go twice as fast, and I'm sure you could use the moral support."

Tana blinked back the tears that had sprung to her eyes. "I'm sure, sweetheart. I'll be fine, believe me. Selene has already promised to help me sort through everything, and we're planning to have a little bit of a girls' weekend while I'm there."

Besides, Tana didn't want Emery to witness her mother falling apart completely as she packed up the life she thought would be hers forever. Even though she and Derek were planning on taking turns sorting through their things, choosing what they wanted and either donating or selling the rest, Tana knew the ghost of their relationship would be keeping a watchful eye on her the entire time, taunting her with the memories of what could have been.

"Okay…" Emery sounded uncertain. "But you can call me whenever you like, Mom, okay? Even if it's the middle of the night and you just need someone to talk to. My phone is always on ring. For you."

She emphasized the last two words, leaving their true meaning unspoken.

"Emery." Tana's voice was soft but firm. "You need to call your father, okay? What happened between us has nothing to do with you, and he loves you more than anything. I'm sure it's killing him that you're refusing to talk to him."

A heavy silence fell over the line for so long that Tana feared her daughter had hung up. Most of their phone conversations since Tana had broken the news of the divorce to her and Derek's only child were fraught with emotion, and Emery hadn't held back about her feelings for her father. And while Tana silently agreed with most of Emery's points— that Derek's selfish behavior had broken up their family, that he was making an embarrassment of himself by parading around Hollywood with a woman young enough to be his daughter—Tana had remained steadfast in her belief that Emery needed her father, and he needed her. When Emery got married someday, she was determined that Derek was going to walk their daughter down the aisle like he had always dreamed about, even if it meant Tana's own day was tainted by his presence. This wasn't about her anymore—as a mother, Tana's main priority, now and always, was her daughter's happiness.

"I have nothing to say to him," Emery bit out. "Nothing good, at least. I'm telling you, if I call him right now, it's only going to make things worse." She lapsed into silence once more, though Tana could hear the occasional sniffle on the other end of the line that felt like a knife to her heart.

She sighed heavily. She could only hope that Derek would someday realize the havoc he was wreaking on their daughter—and her future trust in men—but right now, at least if the tabloid photos she saw at the grocery store were to be believed, he was too busy cavorting around Los Angeles with his much younger flame.

"Okay," she finally said. "But if you want to talk to him, please know that you have my full support."

Just then, Tana spotted Reed's golf cart pulling into the inn's small parking lot—the island's residents weren't permitted to own vehicles, so the carts were their preferred method of travel. Her stomach flipped slightly as she saw him emerging from the cart, the white T-shirt he was wearing doing little to mask the muscles in his arms. He pushed his sunglasses onto his dark hair and glanced toward the inn, giving her a wave and a grin when he spotted her through the window.

She said goodbye to Emery and hung up with the promise that they would talk again soon, then quickly smoothed her hair and checked her makeup in her compact mirror before rising from the chair to greet Reed at the door. Despite Tana's insistence that she would be fine making the trip herself, Reed had insisted on accompanying her to the airport. He must have sensed that she needed some company to take her mind off the dreaded few days ahead, and to be honest, Tana hadn't put up much of a fight. She was secretly excited—and nervous—to be spending some alone time with him, even if it was just for the ferry ride to the mainland.

"Hey," he said when she opened the door and stepped back to allow him inside. He gave her an easy smile that caused yet another stomach flip, though Tana did her best to ignore it. "You ready for this?"

"Absolutely not," Tana said with a sigh, then grabbed the handle of her suitcase and gestured toward the door. "After you."

CHAPTER 3

*E*die Dawes settled herself behind the counter at Antiques on the Bay, the shop she had owned and operated for twenty years, and wriggled her feet out of her strappy teal sandals. She had always loved a stylish shoe, but these days, stylish shoes didn't love her back. Edie supposed that was one of the casualties of growing old, although she absolutely refused to follow in her own mother's footsteps and wear orthopedic shoes with socks tugged up to her knees. She could only imagine the look on her Johnny's face if she would have shown up to one of their weekly dinner dates in old-woman attire.

Not that she was old, thank you very much.

And not that Johnny was around anymore to tease her.

Edie sighed heavily as she slipped on her glasses and poured herself a glass of the sweet tea she always kept in a pitcher near her desk. Even though twenty years had passed since her beloved husband took his last breath, the pain of losing him was ever-present, like an unwelcome solicitor who insisted on knocking on her door first thing each morning. It was in every beat of her heart, every rise and fall of her chest, every shadow that lurked in the corner of her eye. She loved him, and she always would.

But somewhere along the way, she had also started loving someone else.

"Foolish," she muttered to herself, tugging a box of old photographs someone had donated to the shop toward herself and beginning to sift through them. Even though she had never quite understood their appeal, black-and-white photos, many of them taken before she was even born, were always a huge hit with the antiquing crowd.

Picking up an image of a young woman wearing a Victorian-style dress and scowling at the camera, Edie scrutinized it for a moment before setting it down and moving on to the next—a smiling teenage couple from the 1920s, him with slick-backed hair and a collared shirt, her with a stylish bob and headband. She scowled at the girl, then slapped the photo onto her desk hard enough to make a nearby pile of papers scatter.

"Why now?" she said to herself, staring down at the girl's youthful innocence. "Why after all these years has he decided to dredge up the past?"

Edie didn't know anything about Penny—in all the years she'd known Henry, he'd never uttered a word about her. Which was, of course, typical Henry. But it didn't take a genius to figure out that she was a former girlfriend, at the very least... and she had made enough of an impact on Henry that now, sixty years later, he still carried a torch for her.

A strange feeling flitted through Edie's chest, and she rubbed at it, her lips pursed in confusion. The feeling almost—*almost*—reminded her of... jealousy? How ridiculous, she thought, shaking her head and then taking a long sip of tea to distract herself. She was seventy-four years old, for goodness' sake. The time for jealousy had come and gone many sunsets ago.

But even she couldn't deny that the idea of Henry reuniting with this Penny, whoever she was, unsettled Edie far more than she cared to admit. Especially since she had thought that he was finally beginning to acknowledge the feelings that had been growing between them for years. What had started out as a friendship had blossomed into something more, and Edie was positive that he knew it too. Sometime in the past twenty years, their casual evening chats on the inn's porch had grown more intimate, with shared looks and subtle touches on the hand or the knee that couldn't be mistaken for anything but genuine feelings.

That's what Edie had thought, at least, until Penny's photos resurfaced and Henry seemed to have finally stepped right off the edge of sanity. He was a basket case these days, more so than usual, and most of the island's residents, who already steered clear of him, kept an even wider berth than they normally did.

Edie knew that Henry was misunderstood, a gentle soul with a gruff, grouchy exterior he used to keep other people at arm's length. It was a defense mechanism, a wall designed to keep anyone from getting close to him—though for the life of her, she had no idea why he had erected it in the first place. Edie had truly believed that she would be the one to finally tear it down—in fact, she was positive that suffering a stroke would cause him to reevaluate his life, and finally admit to her that she was more than just his friend.

Then Penny came along and ruined the whole thing.

And Edie was absolutely *not* jealous. How could

she be? The girl was a ghost, even if she still lived and breathed and walked this earth, oblivious to the fact that an eighty-three-year-old man on an island in the middle of the Atlantic was still in love with her.

The bell above the shop's door chimed, and Edie stood to greet the pair of middle-aged women wearing breezy summer dresses and floppy sunhats. The island was on the edge of tourist season, and soon the streets would be packed with vacationers from all walks of life. Some of the island's residents preferred the solitude of the winter months, but Edie loved watching the children building sandcastles and the young couples strolling along the boardwalk while holding hands. It made her feel less lonely somehow.

"Welcome to Antiques on the Bay," she said, approaching the two women with a smile. They were admiring a brass lamp with a beautiful gold-threaded shade, their heads bent together over the price tag.

"That's an absolute steal," one of them said to Edie, giving her a friendly smile. "And this is a lovely shop. Are you the owner?"

"The one and only." Edie glanced down at her feet and realized that she had forgotten to slide her sandals back on. "I guess you could say I consider it more of my home. Today I'm going for barefoot casual."

She gestured to her feet and shared a laugh with the two women before the bell chimed a second time and an older couple with sun-kissed skin and matching pastel polo shirts strolled in. They made a beeline for Edie's collection of antique tables in the back corner of the shop, and after making sure that no one needed her help, Edie settled herself in behind her desk once more.

As she strapped her sandals back on, she caught sight of the framed photo on her desk of her three children—Reed, the baby and her only son, and her older daughters, Laurie and Karina. The photo was taken when the three of them were children, sitting on the concrete wall at their old home and laughing while popsicles melted down their hands, happier times that Edie missed with every fiber of her being. But when Johnny died and she decided to move to the island for a fresh start, where every day wasn't a reminder of all that she had lost, she was able, in time, to pick up the pieces and settle into a new kind of happiness. In the twenty years since then, the island had become her home, a part of her soul and her identity, and she couldn't imagine living anywhere else.

But sometimes she wished Reed hadn't come with her.

She knew he was happy—he, too, had become enchanted with life on Dolphin Bay—but she always felt like he had given up his chance for a family by following her here, to practically the middle of nowhere. He'd never been able to find a woman he wanted to settle down with, let alone one he'd fallen in love with, and now, Edie was terrified that he was about to have his heart broken.

Because she saw the way he looked at Tana when he thought no one else was watching. While Tana was a wonderful girl, and quickly becoming a close friend of Edie's, she was in the middle of a messy divorce and had probably decided to close off her heart for a while. Not that Edie could blame her in the least—she would have done the same thing in Tana's shoes. Heck, she was about to do the very same thing with Henry. A woman had to protect herself.

The older couple finished examining Edie's selection of tables and then waved to her as they made their way to the door, but the pair of women approached, one of them holding the brass lamp. "I just couldn't let this slip away," she said as she dug a wallet out of her beach bag and handed Edie her credit card. "I have to say," she added, looking around the shop while Edie rang up her purchase, "I've been in a lot of antique shops over the years, and this one is by far the most well-organized. Usually everything is all jumbled together and you can barely squeeze through all the items for sale without tripping over something or knocking it off a shelf."

"I tried to make it look more like a home," Edie said, handing the customer her credit card and a receipt. "I figure if I'm going to spend the rest of my days here, I might as well be comfortable."

"Sounds like a good plan to me," the woman said, hoisting the lamp into her arms. "But it's a beautiful day outside," she added as she turned to leave. "Make sure you don't work too hard." Then they were gone, leaving Edie alone with her thoughts once more.

She barely had time to settle back into her chair when the door chimed again. Edie automatically glanced at the clock, hoping it was near closing time. While she loved her shop, the older she got, the longer each day felt. Eventually she would have to cut back her hours, but Edie was always a firm believer that staying active was good for the body, mind, and soul. As her mother always said, "I'll rest when I'm dead."

The sound of a cane thumping against the shop's floor drew Edie out of her thoughts, and she looked away from the clock to greet her next customer. Except it wasn't a customer—it was Henry, stepping foot inside her shop for the first time in as long as she could remember.

"What are you doing here?" she said automatically, frowning at him as he limped up to the desk. His face was pinched with the effort, but Henry would never admit to anything resembling weakness or vulnerability. She hurried around the desk to grab him a chair, but he waved her off with a grunt.

Then he fixed his piercing green eyes on hers and said, "I want you to know, Edie, that I have to do this." His voice held its usual curmudgeonly tone, but this time, it was much softer around the edges. He kept his gaze steady on hers, and she could feel a blush creeping up her cheeks.

A blush? What was she, fourteen? She inwardly scolded herself for being ridiculous, and then folded her arms over her chest.

"I have no idea what you're blabbering on about, Henry. Did you take too many heartburn pills again?"

That usually elicited a half-smile from Henry— which equaled a full-on belly laugh for most people —but he merely remained silent, those penetrating eyes still focused on her face. "You know perfectly well what I mean, Edie. I *have* to do this. I have to find her. If I don't... I can't move forward with my life."

There it was. The truth. That old bag of bones —*her* old bag of bones—was in love with a ghost from his past. All those wasted evenings she had spent with him, watching the sunset from the swing-for-two on the inn's porch, her hand resting lightly on his. All those wasted afternoons she'd spent picnicking with him near the shore, watching the waves roll in.

All those wasted feelings.

"Why?" The question was out of her mouth before she could stop it. "I thought..." Her voice trailed off, the words caught in her throat. She cleared it loudly, trying to dislodge the lump that had settled there, and said, "I thought I knew you, Henry."

He gave her a sad smile. "You couldn't possibly know me, Edie. No one does. Not anymore."

CHAPTER 4

*S*ummer 1957

Henry Turner sat behind the inn's front desk, staring at the piece of paper in front of him and chewing anxiously on the end of his pencil. He had barely glanced up all day, other than to check in a family of four to their rooms and call in the weekly order for the grocers. Once again, he ran his eyes down the two columns he had made on the page; the one on the left was filled with line after line of his neat handwriting. The one on the right only held a single word.

"Pros of staying on the island," he muttered to himself for what had to be the hundredth time that day as he started reciting the left-hand column once again. "The inn. My friends. My family. The beach.

The boardwalk. The seagulls. The smell of the ocean in the morning. Evening bonfires in the sand…"

The list went on and on, one reason after another for why Henry wanted—no, *needed*—to stay in Dolphin Bay.

When he finished reading them, he turned once more to the right-hand column. "Pros of moving to New York City," he said, then let his eyes trail over the five letters written there, the ones that contained his heart and soul in every stroke of his pencil.

Penny.

Was there even a decision to be made, really? As much as the thought of leaving the island tore his heart out, he could never even begin to fathom a future without Penny. And he knew she felt the same way about him—if he told her he wanted to stay on the island, she would set aside her dreams and stay too. He couldn't let that happen, not after seeing the way her eyes had lit up with excitement at the prospect of going to school, of making a life for herself outside of being a homemaker and mother. He would never stomp on her dreams, or allow her to give them up for him.

So it was with a heavy heart that he would leave Dolphin Bay. Because the truth of the matter was simple: he loved the island, but he loved Penny more.

"Son? Can I talk to you for a few minutes?"

Henry hadn't even heard his father come in, and he quickly slid his pros and cons list underneath the inn's ledger so he wouldn't catch sight of it. Right now, he didn't feel the need to confide in his parents about what was happening with Penny. They planned to run the inn for at least another decade, giving everyone time to figure out what would come next. While they would find out sooner rather than later that their only child was planning to leave the island, Henry was already drained, physically and mentally, from the weight of the decision he'd had to make.

He needed time to gather his thoughts. And tell Penny the good news, of course.

Henry followed his father into the inn's cozy library, which his mother had carefully decorated with comfortable leather sofas, sturdy oak book-shelves, and a breathtaking watercolor painting of the Dolphin Bay harbor. It was Henry's favorite place in the inn, and he loved spending hours curled up on the sofa with Penny, reading books or watching a variety program on the new television set his parents had recently purchased.

"Sit down, please," his father said, gesturing to a pair of leather armchairs in the corner of the room.

He lowered himself into one and watched his father do the same, grimacing as he settled onto the cushion—the older man's back was probably acting up again, Henry thought with a sympathetic wince. He'd been having sharp pains in his back for months now, and even though Henry's mother had been trying to convince him to see a doctor, he held the old-school view that doctors were only for sick people. "I'm healthy as a horse, Marta," he liked to say, puffing on his ever-present cigarette. And he was as stubborn as a mule, too, so there was no convincing him otherwise.

His father stared down at his hands for a long moment while Henry waited somewhat impatiently. Now that he had made his decision about New York, he was itching to tell Penny. He hadn't seen her since the night of their almost-engagement, and he was eager to slide that beautiful sapphire ring back in his pocket and try again.

But when his father finally looked up and met Henry's gaze, he was alarmed to see that the older man's face was lined with sadness. "There's no use beating around the bush," he said, his green eyes, so like Henry's own, looking every which way but at his son. "I'm not well, Henry. The doctors... they say I don't have much longer. A couple months, in the best-case scenario."

His hands automatically reached for the pack of cigarettes in his breast pocket, but he stopped himself, shaking his head angrily. "Darn things. Doc Halley says they're the most likely cause of all this." He rubbed his chest. "Something about filling up my lungs with garbage. Who knew." He lifted one shoulder in a shrug.

Henry reeled back in shock. Had his father, the man who had assumed an almost superhero presence in Henry's life over the years, just told him that he was dying? Henry shook his head vigorously, certain he had misheard. Certain the doctor was wrong. Doc Halley might be the island's longtime family physician, a grandfatherly man each and every resident trusted with their life, but even he was bound to make a mistake once in a while. Stephen Turner was a young man, barely in his fifties, and now, here he was, sitting in front of Henry and trying to tell him that in a mere few months he would be just... gone?

It was unfathomable.

"No." Henry's voice was so choked he could barely force out the word. He leapt to his feet and hurried to his father's side, dropping before him on both knees and folding his hands as if in prayer. "No, it isn't true. We'll get a second opinion, find a doctor on the mainland who specializes in such things. We'll..."

Henry's voice trailed off as he cast his eyes

around the room frantically, as if the tall book-shelves or the drapes fluttering gently around the open window would hold some type of answer. "We'll…"

"I've done everything I can, son." Henry's father laid a hand on his shoulder and squeezed; when he glanced up, he saw that the older man's eyes were shining with tears. "I've seen the specialists, done the tests. The truth is the truth, and there's no changing that."

His voice faltered for a moment, and he took a handkerchief out of his pocket and handed it to Henry, who realized for the first time that his cheeks were wet. He swiped away the tears angrily, then leapt to his feet and began pacing around the room, his mind whirling as he tried to come up with some way—*any* way—that he could get out of this mess. That he could turn back the clock to five minutes ago, when he was still blissfully unaware that the most important man in the world to him was telling him that he wouldn't be around for any of the mile-stones that Henry had yet to reach in his life. His wedding day. The birth of his first child. His first home.

His father would miss all of it.

"I'm sorry." His father lowered his head and twid-dled his fingers in his lap. "I wish I didn't have to tell this to you, son, but now that I'm not going to be here anymore, you're going to have to become the man of the house. Your mother... she isn't taking the news well, and you know how fragile her health has always been. When I'm gone, I want you to take care of her. With that being said, the time has come."

Henry watched as his father removed a folded piece of paper from his pocket and held it out to him. "This here is the deed to the inn. You are now the owner/operator. I only hope..."

His voice became strangled once more, and he took a moment to compose himself before adding, in a soft voice that held in it all the pain in the world, "I only hope you love and care for this beautiful place as much as I have. Good luck, son, and Godspeed. I might not be watching you from here on earth, but rest assured that I'll always be with you."

And with that, the older man struggled to his feet, clapped his only son on the shoulder, and quietly left the room. Henry dropped back into the leather armchair, the deed to the inn trembling in his hand, and gazed out the window at the blue-gray waters until the sky lit up coral with the setting sun and darkness began to fall over the island once more.

CHAPTER 5

"*H*ere you go, Ms. Martin. I hope you have a pleasant trip."

The airline agent at the ticketing counter handed Tana her boarding pass and then tagged her luggage before lifting it onto the conveyer belt. Tana felt her eyes glaze over as she smiled automatically at the woman and tucked the pass into her purse.

"Thanks, I'm sure I will."

After all, a trip to California *sounded* appealing—maybe the woman would like to go in her place? Anything to avoid stepping back into the house that held so many memories of the marriage she'd thought was a happy one.

"You okay?"

Tana felt a reassuring hand on her shoulder and turned to find Reed peering down at her, his pale blue eyes warm with concern. He'd done his best to distract her from what was to come on their ferry ride and then the taxi drive to the airport, asking her questions about the inn's upcoming renovations and entertaining her with stories about his childhood, but even she had to admit that she was lousy company right now. Most of her answers were one-word, if she responded at all, and by the end of the trip, Reed joined her in staring out the taxi window wordlessly, though as they neared the airport, he rested his hand on hers and gave it a gentle squeeze, as if to say, *I'm here. It's going to be okay.*

Was it, though? Pretending Derek didn't exist— and doing her best not to picture him wrapped in Lucia's arms—was much easier from three thousand miles away. Being back in Los Angeles, back at the scene of his crime...

Tana blinked furiously, trying to beat back the tears, and took several deep breaths to rein in her emotions. The last thing she needed was to have a full-on breakdown right here in the middle of the airport, surrounded by excited families and couples preparing to jet off on their summer vacations.

"Hey. Look at me." Reed tipped her chin up to meet his gaze, their faces so close that for a fleeting moment Tana was positive he was going to kiss her. Her heart stalled and then began beating wildly as she tried to imagine what it would feel like to have his lips on hers, and she was just trying to figure out the last time she'd popped a stick of gum in her mouth when he backed up a step, though his eyes never left her face.

"This is going to suck. There's no getting around that." Reed gave her a small smile. "But you know my number, and if you need anything while you're there, even if it's just someone to vent to, call me anytime, even if it's the middle of the night. I mean that, Tana."

And she could tell by the sincerity in his tone that he truly did. Before she could stop herself, she stepped forward and pulled him into a hug, wrapping her arms around his torso and holding onto him as if he were a life jacket thrown to her in the raging seas.

His arms tightened around her waist and he dropped his chin to the top of her head, resting it there. As they stood together, the hustle and bustle of the airport dropped away, and Tana was only aware of the steady rise and fall of his breathing and the subtle beating of his heart.

"Thank you," she whispered, finally breaking the hug. She hitched her purse over her shoulder and managed a smile as he took a few steps back, arms now hanging at his sides. "I'll see you when I get back, okay?"

"I'll be here," he said, then shoved his hands into his pockets, his eyes on her as she made her way to the escalator that would take her to the departure gates. She stepped onto it, and just before she rose out of sight, he raised his hand and gave her a single wave before turning on his heel and walking away.

"You're awfully quiet tonight."

Edie glanced at her son in concern as they both ate their spaghetti in silence. Reed didn't have much of an appetite—which was definitely enough to raise his mother's eyebrows—and he realized then that he'd been twirling a massive pile of spaghetti around and around on his fork with no intentions of actually eating it.

"Sorry, bad day at work."

That wasn't a lie—not technically. The early summer season was starting to ramp up, and in the past few years, Reed's business had exploded through word-of-mouth recommendations from happy customers. He was thrilled that Dolphin Bay Adventures, the water sports rental and island tour company he had built from the ground up, was bringing in enough income to make for a comfortable life, but the days could be grueling, to say the least. Today alone, before accompanying Tana to the airport, he had conducted three group kayak tours of the island, causing his arm muscles to ache in protest.

Not to mention Kelly, the assistant he'd hired to help him with the rental aspect of the business, had invited him, yet again, to join her and her friends for a beach barbecue that night. Her not-so-subtle flirtations were starting to grate on his nerves—not only were they completely unprofessional, but he just wasn't interested in dating her, plain and simple.

"I don't believe you." Edie's voice was sharper than usual, causing Reed to look up from his plate with a frown.

"You don't believe me about what?"

Edie set down her fork and crossed her arms over her chest. "You've been running that business for years and you love it—not once have I ever heard you say that you had a bad day. Come on, Reed. Your mother knows you better than that—I did raise you, after all."

She gave him a fierce look, and he automatically quelled under the steely glint in her eye. His mother was the kindest, most generous woman he knew, but she was also a force to be reckoned with, even as she aged.

But a lie was easier to tell than the truth, so he merely shrugged and said, "I have no idea what you're talking about," before shoving the massive forkful of spaghetti into his mouth, cheeks bulging.

"Reed." Edie reached across the table and took his hand. "I was in love with your father, remember? I know how these things work. You have feelings for Tana, and you're bothered that she's back in California."

Sometimes the woman could read minds, he thought with a shake of his head. He toyed with his fork for a long moment, and then finally nodded. "I'm concerned that she and her husband are going to reconcile. They have a history together, and she and I have known each other for what, a month? That can hardly compare to twenty years of marriage and a kid."

Then he gave a rough laugh. "I don't even know why I'm telling you all this, anyway. Tana and I are friends—she hasn't given me any indication that she's interested in being more. She isn't even divorced yet, for crying out loud."

A look of fury flashed across Edie's face, but for the life of him, Reed had no idea why.

"And have *you* ever given *her* any indication that

you're interested in being more?" she demanded. "Love is a two-way street, Reed, and that woman is nursing a broken heart. There's no way she's going to go out on a limb and tell you how she feels about you because she doesn't want to get hurt again. But I see it, Reed, I do—I can tell by the way she looks at you that she desperately wants to be more, even if she hasn't admitted that to herself yet."

Edie took a deep breath. "To tell you the truth, I've been watching you and Tana from the sidelines for weeks now, and I've been worried sick that you're going to have your heart broken. But you know what? If you don't pursue her, if you don't see what this could lead to, then your heart will be broken just the same. Because I can't imagine anything worse than falling for someone and watching them run into the arms of another woman, someone they haven't even *seen* for sixty years—"

Reed stared at his mother, baffled, as she stopped speaking abruptly and pressed her fingers to her lips as if to stifle her words. Somewhere along the way, this conversation had steered itself away from him. He mentally reviewed what she had said, and then leaned forward slowly, locking his eyes with hers.

"Is this about Henry?"

There could be no other explanation, and if Edie

wasn't going to let her son get away with a lie, then he *absolutely* wasn't going to let her do the same.

"That old kook?" Edie guffawed, just a little too loudly, and smacked Reed on the hand. "You better get your brain checked, boy, because I think you're losing it." She narrowed her eyes at him, though the expression couldn't hide the color now staining her cheeks. "Shame. I figured at my age, I'd be the one to lose my faculties first."

"Nope. No way. You aren't getting away with this one." Reed narrowed his eyes right back at his mother. "You're in *love* with Henry?"

So Daphne had been right after all—while Reed had finally conceded that Edie and Henry were closer than casual friends, he refused to entertain the notion that the two of them were in love. It was ridiculous, mainly because Henry was more or less a hermit who seemed incapable of even *liking* anyone, let alone loving them. And then he recalled the bundle of old photos Henry had saved for six decades, lovingly tied with a fraying, faded red ribbon.

Maybe the grouchy old man was capable of love after all.

And maybe his mother was upset that he planned to reach out to his old flame, whoever and wherever she may be.

"I'm not in love with him." Edie was staring at her water, tracing her finger down the line of condensation that had formed on the glass. "Or maybe I am, I don't know." She gave her son a desperate look. "Sometimes I don't even *like* the old bag of bones. How could I possibly love him?" She pressed her hands to her cheeks, which were still flaming. "And how am I sitting here at seventy-four years old, having a conversation about this with my son?"

"You're never too old for love," Reed said, taking his mother's hand and giving it a gentle squeeze. "We can't help who we fall for any more than we can help who our family is. I'm just sorry that Tana found those old photographs of Penny in the first place. If she hadn't, and if I hadn't encouraged her to talk to Henry about them..."

He took a deep breath, suddenly aware that he had played no small part in his mother's current heartache. "None of this would have happened."

"Oh, honey, that's not the way it works."

Reed glanced up at his mother to find her shaking her head vigorously, her dangling turquoise earrings slapping against her cheeks. "Henry didn't put those photos in his drawer and forget about them—he knew they were there, and no amount of pretending that they weren't was going to change that. Penny may have left Henry, in one way or another, but he clearly never left her. And that's just something I'm going to have to deal with."

She gave him a soft smile. "Besides, I went through the pain of losing your father. Nothing— and I mean *nothing*—in this life is ever going to hold a candle to that. If I could get through that and come out the other side, then this old ticker of mine can get over all this silly business with Henry."

The sadness in her eyes was replaced with fierce-ness as she jabbed her fork in the direction of Reed's plate. "Now eat your spaghetti and change the subject. I was much happier when we were talking about *your* love life."

CHAPTER 6

*T*ana stood in the middle of her beautiful living room, decorated in the soft blues and greens and tans of the Southern California shoreline, and stared at the oversized wedding photo hanging on the wall above the fireplace. They'd hired a talented photographer for the evening who had captured all of the special moments, but this one—a candid shot of her wrapped in Derek's arms—had always been her favorite. They were nose-to-nose, grinning at each other like a couple of giddy schoolkids, their eyes lit up with the promise of a bright and happy future.

Now, twenty-some years later, her husband was probably holed up in a hotel room somewhere with a sultry Italian actress half his age while she stood here alone, picking up the pieces of what should have been. Strangely, she wasn't crying—and hadn't since she'd stepped out of the airport and taken a cab through LA's infamous traffic to their Beverly Hills home, a recent purchase that had, until a month ago, been her pride and joy. Perhaps she was all cried out, having spent countless nights on the inn's porch, tucked into her favorite worn-out wicker chair as she gazed out at the churning sea.

Or perhaps she was beginning to move on. She felt it in her bones, barely perceptible but growing with each passing day. Dolphin Bay had a healing effect on her soul, and the people she met there, the old relationships rekindled and the new ones blossoming, made her feel alive in a way she hadn't in a very long time.

Even so, Tana knew that the next few days were going to be nothing short of torture. As she looked around the house, with its grand staircase, high ceilings, and chic furnishings she had painstakingly picked out with the help of a team of interior decorators, she had no idea where to begin. How did one go about packing up the broken pieces of the life they thought they'd live forever?

A series of soft knocks drew her attention to the front door, and when she crossed the spacious foyer to open it, she saw her next-door neighbor and friend Selene standing there with several boxes and rolls of garbage bags.

"What are you doing here already? I wasn't expecting you until later tonight," Tana said in surprise, then pulled her friend into a hug.

Selene was just about the only thing she missed about life in California—the woman was spunky and fun, always up for a laugh and a good time. In the weeks since Derek's betrayal had come to light, she had also proven herself to be a true friend, something Tana had learned were rare gems in this world. Selene was the only person in her former life who had even bothered calling to check in on Tana—so much for the other "wives of important men" she'd met during Derek's rise to fame in the entertainment industry. She hadn't heard a peep from them, and knew she never would.

"I figured you could use a friend the second you got home." Selene deposited the rolls of garbage bags in the foyer. "You know how often I go through the men in my life, right? I've become an expert at taking out the trash." She laughed then, loud and long, and though her eyes were sparkling, Tana could detect a hint of hurt behind them that she'd never noticed before. Probably because Tana had never been hurt—now that she knew what it felt like, though, she could spot a kindred soul a mile away.

Still, she was incredibly grateful for the company, and told Selene that as they carried the bags and boxes up to Tana's bedroom—she figured she'd start with the most painful place, rip the bandage off as fast as possible. But when they got there, she stopped in the doorway so abruptly that Selene bumped into her from behind and sent the boxes toppling to the floor.

"What's wrong?" she asked, peering over Tana's shoulder. And then she said, more quietly, "Oh," when the answer became obvious.

Tana's bedroom had been stripped of all things Derek. His side of the bed was completely empty—the book on his nightstand was gone, along with his reading glasses, the pair of slippers he kept under the bed, and even his pillowcase. A quick peek into the room's walk-in closet revealed top and bottom rows of empty hangers, shoeboxes removed from their cubby holes, and a bare hook where the vintage lounge jacket Tana had gifted him on their twentieth wedding anniversary used to hang. The only thing left, sitting in its tiny black velvet box in the middle of the floor, as if to taunt her, was his wedding ring.

"That jerk." Selene's voice was practically shaking with rage on Tana's behalf. She stomped into the closet, grabbed the ring box, and shoved it deep inside Derek's nightstand drawer, out of sight. "How could he do this to you?"

"No, it's—it's fine." Once the initial shock had set in, Tana realized she was glad that Derek's things were no longer around. "Honestly, Selene," she added when her friend gave her a dubious look. "It's better this way—now I can focus on boxing up my own things."

She stepped into the room with a sigh, averting her eyes from Derek's side of the bed. Then she headed for the closet, Selene at her heels, and gazed at the rows of beautiful designer clothes and shoes she'd purchased over the years. At the time, they had seemed like necessary expenses—keeping up with the Joneses was goal number one in a town like Beverly Hills—but now, it just seemed frivolous. All those thousands of dollars could have gone toward renovating the inn instead, or helping Tana build a life outside of the one she'd known with Derek.

"You have such beautiful things," Selene murmured, running her hands along a sapphire cocktail dress that Tana had worn to the premiere of Derek's first movie. She remembered how nervous she'd been walking the red carpet for the first time, terrified that she'd trip and smash her face into the ground while the paparazzi cameras clicked away and she ended up on the front page of some tabloid the next morning. But the evening had gone off without a hitch, and seeing the years Derek had spent toiling over his screenplay, never giving up on his dream, finally coming to fruition had made for a magical night.

After the movie was over and the requisite after-parties had wrapped up, Tana and Derek had driven to a 1950s-style diner in Hollywood that they both loved, gorging themselves on burgers and shakes while recounting everything that had led them to this point. Tana had been deliriously happy for him that night; little did she know that the career he'd fought for so long to have would eventually lead to their undoing.

"You can have it." Tana slid the dress off the hanger and draped it over Selene's arms. "It would look stunning with your hair."

When Selene began to protest, she shook her head resolutely. "Consider it a thank-you for all that you've done for me over the past few weeks. Besides, I have no use for it anymore. I'm living the island life now—we're all about beachy chic." She grinned at her friend, realizing that the smile was genuine.

Selene returned the smile, sighing with happiness as she held the dress up to her body in the mirror and examined her reflection from every angle. Then she turned back to Tana and grabbed her wrist, holding it firmly in her hand so Tana was forced to look her in the eye.

"You're a stronger woman than I am, Tana. I'm in awe of you—most people would have curled up in a ball and never left their bed after what happened to you. You—you've made a new life for yourself, and I have to say, something about you seems... different. You have this glow about you that I've never seen before." Selene gave her a sharp look, and then her eyes lit up with excitement. "You've met someone!"

"I have not *met* someone," Tana said with a laugh, though her mind immediately flashed to an image of Reed at the airport, right before she left for California.

"You're lying." Selene's voice was triumphant. She slid the dress back onto its hanger and dropped to the floor, arranging herself into a cross-legged position and patting the carpet beside her. "Come on. Spill it. I've been going through a dry spell lately, so I need every last juicy detail."

"Sorry to disappoint you, but I don't have a single juicy detail to share." Tana nudged her friend aside and reached for a garbage bag, shaking it open before considering the rows of shoeboxes lined up on the closet floor. "Now come on. Help me decide which things I should keep and which I should donate. Feel free to take whatever you like, too. It's the least I can do for all the help you've given me."

It was also her sneaky way of distracting Selene from asking more uncomfortable questions Tana didn't want to answer, she thought as her friend squealed with delight and made a beeline for the cashmere sweaters.

ALL IN ALL, the evening had been a success, Tana thought as she waved to Selene and closed the door behind her. It was hard to believe she'd only left Dolphin Bay earlier that day—but with the time change and Selene's help, she'd made a major dent in her packing. Her bedroom was currently filled with dozens of bags earmarked for charity, along with a much smaller pile of clothes and other personal belongings that Tana would be shipping back to Maine. Tomorrow they would start tackling the rest of the house, along with the help of a designer furniture reseller whose help Tana had enlisted. The man would be hauling most of her furniture back to his swanky shop, and she would get a tidy cut of the profits when it sold.

But that could all wait until tomorrow. Right now, Tana wanted nothing more than to curl up on

the sofa, flip through Netflix until she found something that interested her, and eat a few more slices of
the pizza she and Selene had ordered before conking
out for the night.

She grabbed her plate and added two slices of
pepperoni, then considered the pizza box for
another moment before sliding two more slices on
top. Then she poured herself a soda and headed for
the couch, settling herself into it with a moan of
exhaustion. Today's work had been draining, both
physically and emotionally, and she could use a nice,
long—

The sound of a car door slamming interrupted
Tana's thoughts, and she flicked her gaze toward the
window before taking an enormous bite of the
pizza, melted cheese dangling from her lips. A
second car door opened and closed, followed by the
sound of two people talking—a man and a woman.
She couldn't hear their conversation through the
open window, but the woman's Italian accent was
unmistakable.

Derek was here. And he had brought his mistress
with him.

Tana gagged on her slice of pizza, dropping it
back onto the plate as though it had scorched her
and reaching for a napkin. She wiped a smear of
sauce off her chin, her heart racing with a mix of

anxiety and fury. How *dare* he bring her here, to Tana's house? Especially when they had agreed to steer clear of each other during the process of preparing the house for sale. Weren't things painful enough already?

She stomped toward the door, but she didn't have time to yank it open before Derek shoved the key into the lock. His murmur of surprise that the door was unlocked was followed by a look of shock as he pushed it open to find Tana standing there, hands on hips, eyes blazing with fury, errant smear of pizza sauce on her sweatshirt.

"What are you... why are you... how are you?" he spluttered, stepping in front of Lucia, who was standing behind him, looking bored.

The protective move only further raised Tana's ire, but she took three long breaths to steady herself. She was going to be the bigger person here. She was not going to make a scene, no matter how much she would have loved to grab a slice of pizza and smear it all over Lucia's arrogant face. Let the paparazzi take a photo of *that*, she thought smugly.

"What, Derek, get your days mixed up?" she asked coolly, inwardly proud that her voice was steady and calm. She gave Lucia a look of disdain. "And I see you brought your niece—oops, sorry, I meant girlfriend." Derek shot her an annoyed look, but Lucia merely rolled her eyes.

"You are just sorry you are not—how do you say it in English?" The Italian actress smirked at Tana, her expression mocking. "Ah, yes. Young and beautiful." She eyed Tana up and down.

"That's enough." Derek's voice was sharp enough that it surprised both women. "Look, I'm sorry," he said to Tana, looking everywhere but into her eyes. "I just forgot my camera and I needed it for a photo shoot we're doing on set tomorrow. I didn't realize you were here tonight—I marked the days on my calendar, I swear, but I must have made a mistake. But I'm here now, and if it's okay with you, I'll just grab the camera and be on my way. I swear you won't see me again after that."

Ever.

The word lingered in the air between them, unspoken, even though Tana knew it wasn't true. While she would have loved nothing more than to push Derek out of her life forever, they had a daughter together, and no amount of animosity toward each other would change that. They would all be in for a lifetime of pain, Emery included, if she and Derek didn't learn to get along. And since there was no better time to start than the present...

"Fine." Tana heaved a sigh and stepped back,

allowing him entry. "You can come in, but please make it quick. I've had a long day, and I'm beat."

She faltered at the sight of Lucia preparing to enter the house behind him—her generosity and good will didn't extend *that* far—but Derek stopped her with a hand on her arm.

"Wait in the car, okay?" Then he closed the door without waiting for Lucia to respond and turned to face Tana with a sheepish expression. "Thanks."

She could tell by the way he shoved his hands deep into the pockets of his jeans that he was nervous, and that hint of vulnerability softened the arch in her back and the stiffness in her shoulders. She was reminded for just a moment of the Derek she knew—or the one she thought she knew, anyway. It was a strangely comforting thought.

"I'll just be a second." He strode down the hallway toward his office, rummaging around inside for a few moments while Tana hovered by the front door, unsure what to do. How was one supposed to act when running into their almost-ex-husband, anyway? In the end, she settled for padding back to the couch, grabbing her plate of pizza, and flipping on the television—after all, why should her plans for the night change?

A minute later, soft footsteps behind the couch drew her attention away from the television—she had been flicking through the shows without really paying attention to what she was doing—and Derek cleared his throat softly.

"Tana?" he said. "May I have a word?"

Tana debated telling him to take a hike, then sighed and turned around to face him. This was for Emery's sake, she reminded herself yet again, remembering the devastation in her daughter's voice when she found out her parents were getting a divorce. The thought made anger knife through her chest once more, and she said, "Yeah, what is it?" with more aggression than she had intended.

Derek winced, but quickly recovered. "I just wanted to say…"

He was clutching the camera strap tightly in one hand; the other was still shoved deep into his pocket. He toyed with the strap for a moment, Tana following the movement of his hand with her eyes— anything to distract herself from his presence. This was the man she'd adored, and now he was standing in front of her, a virtual stranger.

It wasn't supposed to be this way, she wanted to scream. *We were supposed to grow old together, and you ruined it, Derek. You ruined everything.*

He cleared his throat again, softer this time, drawing her attention back up to his familiar face, once so beloved. "I just wanted to say goodbye."

Then he was gone, heading for the door without looking back. Tana stared after him, long after the door had clicked shut, long after the car engine started and faded into silence as her husband drove away with a woman in the passenger seat who wasn't her.

And never would be again.

She turned back to the television, catching sight of her phone as she did so and remembering what Reed had said to her at the airport.

If you need anything while you're there, even if it's just someone to vent to, call me anytime, even if it's the middle of the night. I mean that, Tana.

Glancing at the clock, Tana calculated the time in Maine. And then, before she could convince herself otherwise, she picked up the phone and began to dial.

CHAPTER 7

*H*e didn't like it. He didn't like it one bit.

Henry Turner leaned heavily on his cane as he watched the men traipse into the inn, carrying armloads of equipment and sullying his hardwood floors with their dirty work boots. They stacked their supplies in his living room, and he let his eyes roam over the hammers and nails and wooden boards and paint cans, his heart pounding a little harder than it usually did.

What if they ruined it? What if they ruined everything?

He barely trusted anyone else with the upkeep of his beautiful inn over the decades, preferring to do as much as he could on his own.

And look where that got you.

Henry squashed the voice in the back of his head

that was always so insistent. It was like a devil on his shoulder, prodding him to do the things he didn't want to. Like agreeing to allow his great-niece Tana to handle the renovations to the inn. Like agreeing to allow the inn to be renovated in the first place.

The Inn at Dolphin Bay had been in his family for three generations, but Henry had been the proprietor longer than anyone. When his father had passed away at an age that was far too young, his mother, in her grief and loneliness, was unable to manage the inn on her own. Henry had started out as her partner, but within a year, he had taken over running the place completely while his mother retired to the mainland to live with her sister.

Everything in Henry's life—all the moments, big and small—had occurred right here in these four walls. His first step. His first skinned knee. His first kiss. The first time he learned that he would have to become the man of the family at the tender age of seventeen.

Best not to think about that. Best not to think about *her*.

Henry limped over to the picture window and gazed out over the blue-gray waters of the Atlantic Ocean. The sea always calmed him, centered him, reminded him that no matter what curve balls life threw at him—and there had been many of them lobbed his way, some smacking him squarely in the chest—the island was home, the place he loved more than anything in the world. Second only to the inn, of course. And now this beautiful building that had belonged to his father, and his grandfather before him, was being practically ripped to shreds and rebuilt from the ground up.

Henry could hardly bear it.

"Mr. Turner. How are you doing this morning?"

Henry turned to find Luke, the contractor, grinning widely at him. He felt the urge to give the man's face a good smack, then realized that he currently only had one working hand. And right now, he needed it to grip the cane the doctors and Tana insisted that he use. He supposed he was falling apart right alongside the inn. Fitting, really.

"I'm doing terrible," he said, scowling at Luke, whose smile immediately dimmed. Henry felt slightly ashamed of himself, but quickly tamped down on it. This man was the enemy. "I hope you and your crew know what you're doing. This inn's been in my family for years. *Decades.* You weren't even a glimmer in your parents' eyes when my grandfather built it from the ground up with his own blood, sweat, and tears."

Luke's eyes were soft as he studied Henry's face, and Henry shifted uncomfortably, leaning heavily on his cane as he tried to compensate for the limited mobility in his left leg. He wobbled, almost losing his balance, and the contractor shot out a hand to stop him from falling.

Henry managed to swat it away impatiently before lowering himself into the nearest chair. "I'm fine," he snapped. "I just need some space."

Luke gave him another long look, the kind of look he'd seen in the eyes of many of the island's residents over the years when they saw him.

Sympathy.

He hated it. Didn't need it. Didn't want it.

"Mr. Turner, I can assure you that my crew is the best around. I've spoken with them extensively about the history of your beautiful inn, and each and every one of them is proud to be working to restore it to its former glory. I'm going to do everything I can to ensure that the renovation process is as quick and painless as possible for you. I also understand that this is your home—and at any time, if this all gets to be too much for you and you need a little break, just let me know. I'd be happy to pull my guys away for a few days, or even set you up with some temporary housing at another of the island's hotels—"

"No!"

The word came out as a shout, startling even Henry.

"No," he said, more quietly this time, but forceful nonetheless. "I'm not leaving my home. I haven't left it for eighty-three years, and I'm not going to start now."

"I understand." Luke rested a hand briefly on Henry's shoulder. "All the same, if you need something, please don't hesitate to let me know."

Then he gave Henry a nod and strode toward his men, delivering the day's first instructions as they crowded around him, listening intently. A few were even taking notes on their phones, which eased Henry's fears somewhat. Maybe this would all be okay. Maybe he would no longer have to watch as the inn he had dedicated his entire life to crumbled to the ground around his feet. It had been like watching a beloved relative endure a slow, painful, torturous death.

And now, they were being given a second chance at life.

He should be grateful; he knew that. Instead, he felt sick. Actually, if he thought about it, he'd been feeling sick since yesterday, when Edie had confronted him at the shop. Their encounter had been replaying in his mind ever since, and it had taken every ounce of willpower he possessed not to go to her and apologize.

He had hurt someone he cherished. So what else was new.

But he couldn't make things right with Edie—or with himself—if he didn't finally accept what he had known all along: that he could never truly move on with his life if he didn't find out what had happened to the girl he let slip away. He'd thought about seeking her out many times over the years, but whenever that happened, he managed to convince himself that he didn't have the time, or the means. Now that Tana was here, and willing to help, Henry was left with no more excuses.

It was time to finally address the heartache of his past, once and for all.

He glanced at the clock—it was early in the morning in Dolphin Bay, though Henry was always up before the crack of dawn. That meant it was still the middle of the night in Los Angeles. Tana would probably have her phone off; if she was able to sleep at all, that is. Henry knew a thing or two about heartbreak, and sleep was always the first thing to go.

He cursed under his breath as he raised himself to his feet, using his cane as a guide, and was panting slightly when he finally managed to arrange his body into something resembling an upright position. Then he limped over to the front desk, ignoring the men who were still carrying supplies through the door as he gazed at the bottom drawer, the one that had been a source of anxiety for him for over sixty years. Henry couldn't say for sure why he kept Penny's pictures locked in that drawer for so many decades.

Perhaps they were a reminder of all that he had lost. Or perhaps, he thought, gazing out the window once more at the softly churning ocean, a world away from what he imagined New York City to be like, they were a reminder of all that he had gained.

This time, as he sat behind the desk, he didn't open the drawer and stare at the envelope, yellowed and wrinkled with age. Instead, he picked up the receiver of the old rotary phone he refused to replace for one of those newfangled cellulars and dialed Tana's number.

He breathed a sigh of relief when the call clicked over to voicemail. When the robotic voice urging him to leave a message ended and the line beeped, Henry spoke only six words—but those six words carried with them the disappointments and regrets of a lifetime. And hope, too. For a better future. For peace and true happiness in his final years on earth.

"Penelope Yeats. Journalist. New York City."

"OKAY. I *NEED* TO GET GOING." Tana stared out the window at the sky, inky black with a scattering of stars, and then at the clock on her nightstand. She did a double-take. Was it really 4:00 in the morning? The last time she had stayed up so late was when Emery had a nasty bout of the stomach flu in middle school. But here she was, giggling like a schoolgirl into the telephone while the rest of the world slept peacefully in their beds.

Well, the rest of the world except Reed, of course.

"*You* need to get going?" He chuckled. "What about me? It's 7:00 in the morning. I have an early kayak tour in an hour and I haven't slept a wink. Look what you've done, woman—you've ruined me for the day." His voice was a low rumble, sending a shiver up Tana's spine.

"Watch who you're calling *woman*," she said, flopping back onto her pillow and pulling the cover over herself. "Or else I'll sic Uncle Henry on you. He's got a cane now, and he knows how to use it."

"Yeah, I'm sure he's waving it at the contractors as we speak."

Tana winced at that, then pushed the thought out of her mind. She wouldn't put it past the old man to do just that, but Luke would be able to handle him.

At least she very much hoped so. He seemed capable enough.

"All right, I'm going to let you go." Tana gripped the phone just a little tighter, unwilling to let the call come to an end. "And Reed, again—thank you. This was the perfect distraction."

There was a hesitation on the other end of the line before Reed said, "No problem. Glad I could help." The lightness had disappeared from his tone, though, and Tana quickly realized her mistake.

"You're not a distraction—I'm sorry, that was a terrible way to put it." She could feel her cheeks flaming and was glad for the thousands of miles that separated them. "You're much more than that, Reed. You're—"

She stopped, unsure what to say. There were so many ways she could end that sentence, so many unspoken words that lingered in the air between them during this conversation alone. "You're a wonderful man," she finally settled on. "And I'm so glad to have you in my life."

Truer words had never been spoken. She had only known Reed for a few short weeks, and not only had he answered her call despite the late hour, but he had also stayed on the phone, laughing and chatting with her for hours until the encounter with Derek and Lucia was nothing but a distant memory. A man like that was gold, and Tana knew it.

Reed was silent for a long moment, and Tana held her breath, fearful that she had insulted him beyond the point of repair. Then he exhaled softly and murmured, "I think you're wonderful too, Tana. And I'm looking forward to seeing you when you get home. In the meantime, promise me something, okay?"

"Sure, anything," Tana said without hesitation.

"Promise me that you *will* come home. To the island, that is."

Tana smiled softly. "That's an easy promise to make. I'll see you in a few days, okay?"

They said goodbye and ended the call, and Tana stared at the phone for a few moments before turning it to silent and placing it on the nightstand. As she burrowed deeper into the covers, hoping to get at least a few hours of sleep before enduring another long day of packing, she saw the screen light up with an incoming call. Her heartbeat immediately sped up, but when she saw her uncle's name, she let the call go to voicemail.

Any problems with the inn could wait until later. Right now, she wanted to bask in the memory of Reed's voice until she drifted off to sleep.

CHAPTER 8

*T*ana sat at her kitchen counter, finishing off the last of the pizza and breathing a sigh of relief. It had been a busy morning—she'd finished packing up the bedrooms, then moved on to the closets while the man who owned the designer furniture resale store took inventory of every piece in the house, a process that took hours. Even though Selene had promised to drop by that evening after work to help her finish the last few rooms, Tana didn't know if she had the energy to do much more than climb into bed and take a nice long nap.

But if she wanted to return to Dolphin Bay in three days, she needed to take advantage of every minute remaining on the clock. She tossed the last bite of pizza crust into the empty box and wiped her hands, then headed down the hallway, intent on tackling the coat closet—why she and Derek had needed a coat for every occasion and weather whim was beyond her, since the vast majority of Southern California's days were sunny and gorgeous, but a few of them would come in handy for the island's colder months.

She stopped walking as the implications of that last thought struck her. Her time on the island was meant to be temporary, a few months spent with Uncle Henry to help him recover from his stroke and run the inn. At some point, those few months had stretched and evolved in her mind, and now she was imagining decorating the inn for Christmas, with a roaring fire nearby and a mug of cider in her hand as she gazed out at the snow-covered sand.

And it felt right. Especially if Reed was by her side.

Tana immediately started shaking her head, automatically admonishing herself for the thought, but then stopped. If she had any lingering doubts about her feelings for Reed, they had been completely extinguished during the hours they'd spent on the phone last night. The ease with which they talked, the natural flow of the conversation, the way her heart rate sped up every time his low baritone laugh drifted over the line... that felt right too. There was no sense in denying it any longer.

She was falling for him. Maybe since the first day they'd met. She laughed to herself as she recalled that initial meeting, when she'd been so heartsick at the state of her uncle's beloved inn that she'd mistakenly taken it out on Reed. He'd been a good sport about it then, and in the weeks since, he'd proven himself to be the kind of man who only came around once in a lifetime.

Of course, she'd thought the same thing about Derek, and look how wrong she'd been about that.

Sighing heavily, Tana unfolded a cardboard box and taped it together before writing *Donations* on the side in a black marker. Then she began sorting through the hangers, leaving Derek's things and tossing the majority of her coats into the box. She had almost finished when the doorbell rang, and she threw the last coat on top of the pile and headed for the door, expecting to see Selene.

Instead, Daphne was standing there with a wide grin and a small suitcase at her feet.

"Daph! What are you doing here?" Tana said, delighted.

She ushered her friend into the house and wheeled the suitcase in after her. Then she pulled Daphne into a hug, surprised by how happy she was to see her. Although she and Daphne had been friends throughout their childhood, spending each summer together on the island, they had lost touch when Tana went to college and then moved to Los Angeles with Derek. Daphne had never left the island, and they'd reconnected a few weeks ago, picking up their friendship right where they'd left off, as though they hadn't been apart for more than two decades.

"Remember how you kept inviting me to visit you in Los Angeles that first year you and Derek moved out here? That was, what, twenty-five years ago? Anyway, ta-da!" Daphne spread her arms out wide. "Here I am, in the flesh and ready to party."

"By party, I hope you mean eat a sensible dinner and go to bed early," Tana said, smothering a yawn. "I was up most of the night talking to—"

She stopped speaking and pressed her lips together, but that didn't stop Daphne's eyebrows from shooting up into her hairline. A look of delight spread across her pretty, heart-shaped face as she clapped her hands together and squealed, "I knew it! You and Reed, right? You guys are meant to be together, I'm telling you."

"Whoa. Whoa whoa *whoa.*" Tana held her hands up in a wait-a-minute gesture. "First of all, Reed and I have gone on exactly zero dates—scratch that, he hasn't even *asked* me if I'd be interested in going out on a date. And 'meant to be together?' I've known the guy for all of two seconds."

"More like four weeks, but what does that matter? I'm telling you, Tana—it's meant to be. I can sense these things, and whenever the three of us are spending time together, even though you and I have known each other for forever, I always feel like the third wheel. And I'm perfectly fine with that," she hastened to add when Tana opened her mouth to protest. "Reed's a great guy, and you're an amazing woman—it's only natural that you two would fall for each other."

Despite Daphne's grin, Tana detected an undercurrent of sadness in her tone. She was about to ask her about it, but Daphne kept talking before she could get the words out. "Anyway, I'll bet you all the money in the world that Reed is positively *dying* to ask you out on a proper date but he's worried that you're not ready for it yet. You know, with the divorce and all."

"He's not wrong," Tana admitted, her mind automatically traveling back to her encounter with Derek the previous night. Seeing him with Lucia had hurt. A lot. "I'm not sure that I'm prepared for all that. But Derek is moving on, so I guess..."

She trailed off, her eyes lingering on the framed portrait of her and Derek on their wedding day. She swallowed hard and lowered her gaze to the ground. Daphne stepped forward and pulled her into a hug.

"You know what? We can figure all of this out later—Reed isn't going anywhere. I came here to hit the town, and I'm hoping you'll be my tour guide. I've never been to Hollywood before, and I'm dying to see everything." She pulled a camera out of her suitcase and slung it around her neck, then grabbed a handful of travel brochures she must have picked up at the airport. "I plan to be the most obnoxious tourist in the city. I hope you're okay with that."

"Fine with me." Tana shrugged and picked up one of the brochures that featured splashy pictures of Hollywood, including the Walk of Fame, Grauman's Chinese Theatre, and the famed Hollywood sign. "I probably won't be back in California for a long time, so let's make the most of my last few days here."

She waved the brochure in Daphne's direction. "I promise to be the best tour guide ever if you promise to help me pack up the rest of the house. Then we can fly back to Dolphin Bay together—as much as I'm ready to put all of this behind me, leaving is still going to be hard. And I'd really like to have a friend with me."

"Oh, Tana." Daphne gave her a gentle smile. "Why do you think I'm really here?"

"I can't even remember the last time I had this much fun," Tana said, wiping away tears of laughter as she and Daphne waved goodbye to the Marilyn Monroe and Elvis impersonators and tucked their cameras back into their purses. Hollywood Boulevard was as ridiculous as Tana remembered from the last time she visited—costumed characters strutted down the sidewalks, posing for tourist photos in exchange for tips; people gawked at the stars on the Walk of Fame and pressed their hands into the celebrity handprints at the Chinese Theatre; and open-air double-decker buses filled with tourists snapping photos drove down the street, microphones blaring as the guides entertained them with stories of the town's history.

Tana and Daphne had done it all—stepping into John Wayne's footprints, forever immortalized in concrete, posing beside Lucille Ball's star on the Walk of Fame wearing ridiculous red wigs they'd picked up at the nearby souvenir stand, and taking photos with as many characters as they could find.

As they headed back to the car, Tana's wallet was light—but her heart was lighter. She slung an arm around Daphne's shoulder, knocking them both slightly off balance and eliciting another round of giggles. "Have I mentioned how glad I am that you decided to visit?"

"Only about a hundred times," Daphne said with a wink. "That was a lot of fun, wasn't it?"

"The most I've had in years." Tana opened the car door and slid behind the wheel. "Why don't we run back to the house, put on some nice dresses, and head out to Beverly Hills for a fancy dinner? I know a little place on the corner of Rodeo Drive that has the most amazing Italian food you'll ever eat."

It was also the spot where she and Derek had gone on a hundred date nights over the years, but Tana pushed that thought out of her mind. He had already taken so much from her—she wasn't going to let him ruin her favorite restaurant, too.

"Oh my gosh, that sounds delicious." Daphne settled herself into the passenger seat and pulled the seatbelt across her chest. "Can we invite Selene, too? You've mentioned her so many times I feel like I've already met her."

"I'll shoot her a message right now." Tana tapped out a quick text and sent it to Selene, then pulled into traffic. She had chosen to drive Derek's convertible for the occasion—he'd left it at the house, along with the keys, and Tana had been quick to suggest they take it out for a final spin on this gorgeous day. She raised the roof with the push of a button, and was immediately hit with a burst of warm air and the smell of exhaust fumes from the other cars idling in the bumper-to-bumper traffic.

"This is one of the best things about living on the island," Daphne said, waving her hand in front of her nose to ward off the smell. "No cars equals no noise and no pollution. I don't know how you could stand sitting in traffic like this every day. It would drive me nuts."

"You get used to it," Tana said, but she, too, was daydreaming of the island's fresh, crisp air and sparkling beaches. The residents of Dolphin Bay took pride in their island, and in the weeks that Tana had spent there, she never saw so much as a single piece of litter in the sand or a stray plastic bottle on the sidewalks. It was pristine, and peaceful, and everything she needed right now.

Suddenly, she was feeling homesick—and not for the city she'd lived in for the past twenty-plus years, or the house where she, Derek, and Emery had built precious memories. She glanced at the clock on the dashboard, wondering briefly what Reed was doing and how Uncle Henry was faring at the inn on his own.

Edie had promised to look in on him several times a day while Tana was gone, and she'd even asked Luke, the contractor, to keep an eye on him as well. She'd kept all of that from her uncle, of course —the last thing the stubborn old man wanted was pity or, God forbid, someone to worry about him.

But as she pictured his face, scrunched up in the perpetual frown he wore, she couldn't help but miss him, too. Her mind wandered back to the voicemail he'd left for her during the night, delivered in his usual curt tone. He hadn't even said hello or good-bye, or asked Tana how she was doing. Instead, he'd said only six words: *Penelope Yeats. Journalist. New York City.*

It was, presumably, the only concrete information he had on Penny, and it was little for Tana to go on. But she was determined to track Penny down, no matter how long it took—and she planned to start that very evening, once she and Daphne returned from dinner.

Tana was lost in thoughts about Penny and Henry for the rest of the drive home, and Daphne was quiet too, exhausted from the long trip and the active day. Evening had set in, the sky above them an inky purple as they pulled into the driveway of Tana's house. They hurried inside to change and freshen up, and reconvened in the living room twenty minutes later, dressed for dinner. Selene had agreed to meet them beforehand for drinks, and Tana pulled a bottle of wine out of the kitchen cabinet and poured three generous glasses while Daphne dragged her suitcase up to the spare bedroom.

By the time she returned, Selene was ringing the doorbell, and Tana called, "Come in!" from the kitchen. "This is my old friend Daphne," she said as Selene walked into the room, looking, as always, like a knockout. Her honey-colored hair was pulled into an elegant twist, and her blue eyes were rimmed in charcoal. Even though she was a few years older than Tana, she kept herself fit and could easily pass for a woman ten years younger. Which was probably why she always went for the younger men, Tana thought, covering a smile as her two friends greeted each other with a hug.

"I've heard so much about you," Selene said, pulling away from Daphne and accepting the glass of wine Tana was holding out to her. "Tana's had a rough go of it lately, and I was so happy to hear that she had a friend on the island."

She lowered her voice conspiratorially and flashed Tana an innocent look as she added, "And I think there's someone else, too, but she's refusing to give me any of the details. Care to share?"

"Ah, you mean Reed." Daphne's playful tone matched Selene's as she grinned at Tana, who groaned and grabbed her own wine glass. She took a long sip, pretending not to listen as Daphne filled Selene in on her blossoming friendship with Reed. "And he's gorgeous too," Daphne added, laughing at the look of embarrassment on Tana's face.

"You're making a mountain out of a molehill," she muttered, her cheeks warm. She took another sip of wine just for something to do, swirling the liquid around in her mouth, lips puckering at its strong flavor.

"Honey, a single man in his forties who is looking for a good woman, runs his own successful business, takes care of his mother, *and* is handsome to boot?" Selene said, one eyebrow cocked. "If you don't want him, I do. Book me a ticket on the next plane to Dolphin Bay and I'll see for myself what you're missing out on."

Daphne gasped. "You should definitely come to the island! Not to snag Reed, of course—trust me, he's all Tana's. She just won't admit it yet." A wink at Tana, and then she continued, "But Dolphin Bay is really a special place in the summer. Everyone who visits us falls in love. And you can't beat the food at the diner where I work."

"Or the pastries that Daphne makes." Tana gave her old friend a warm smile. "We've already hired her to provide them for the inn's guests once we're up and running again. Her cherry tarts and home-made fudge brownies are to die for."

"Well I'm sold." Selene held up her wine glass, and the three women clinked them in a toast to friendships, old and new. "Now come on," Selene said, swallowing her sip of wine and setting her glass on the counter. "All this talk of food is making me famished. Let's go enjoy the best Italian food that Southern California has to offer."

CHAPTER 9

"*A*h, Mrs. Martin. So good to see you. Welcome, welcome." Giancarlo, the host at Bella Sera, greeted Tana with a kiss on both cheeks before turning to Selene and doing the same. "Two of the most beautiful women in all of California, right here in the restaurant tonight? What a lucky man I am."

Selene practically melted under the handsome man's attention, but Tana resisted the urge to roll her eyes as, behind her, she heard Daphne stifle a giggle. The host's over-the-top compliments and smooth words were a far cry from the greeting they would receive at Sal's Diner, a Dolphin Bay staple that was a lot more... lived in... than this Beverly Hills hotspot. Its décor featured cracked vinyl seats and worn tabletops, but the food was delicious and the atmosphere homey. Tana loved joining Reed there in the evenings for a chocolate malt and a plate of fries.

"It's *Ms.* Martin now," she said, her smile growing fixed as the host assumed a solemn expression and nodded gravely.

"Ah, yes, I have heard the news. You and Derek were a golden couple, and I was very sorry to hear of your separation." He glanced over his shoulder at the dining tables, suddenly looking a bit uncomfortable, but then his features smoothed out and he smiled at her once more. "I have the best table in the house for you tonight, *signora*. Please come with me."

He turned on one heel and began leading them through the restaurant, toward a round table tucked inside a more private part of the dining room. After pulling out each of their chairs in turn and waiting for the women to take their seats, he offered them menus and poured three glasses of water from the pitcher already sitting on the table. Then he handed them the wine list, which Selene accepted enthusiastically, before bowing and heading back to the front of the restaurant.

"Wow, this place is beautiful," Daphne said, gazing around the room.

The restaurant was decorated in soft cream tones, with candles on each table and a vase with a single red rose in the center. Around them, a who's who of Tinseltown ate and drank while chatting quietly and lingering over the restaurant's famous espresso, ground fresh every day on the premises. Tana couldn't count the number of times she and Derek had been to Bella Sera, whether on romantic date nights or for business meetings with Derek's industry friends and colleagues. It was a place where deals were made, careers were launched, and many came to see and be seen.

And for the first time, Tana felt uncomfortable.

Judging by the look on her face, so did Daphne. She shifted in her chair, adjusting the hem of her black dress around her knees, and toyed with her water glass. Tana saw her sneaking a few glances at the menu—and, more specifically, the prices—and was about to whisper to her that the meal was Tana's treat when Selene announced, loud enough for half the room to hear, "Order whatever you want, ladies! This one's on me. In celebration of Tana's new life as a single woman. Which, from what I hear, isn't going to last long."

She gave Tana an exaggerated wink, and Tana couldn't help but laugh along with her friends before lapsing into an uncomfortable silence again. Even though she recognized more than a few of the diners, she no longer felt like she belonged. She was now a member of the "former wives of Hollywood" club, one that most of the women she knew spent their lives trying to avoid. But Tana had never quite fit in to Derek's world, even though she went the extra mile to be supportive of his career.

Now, she realized as she looked around the restaurant, she would never again have to attend another one of his industry parties, where everyone looked through her the moment they realized she had nothing to offer them. In Dolphin Bay, people were friendly to her because they liked her—even if they didn't know her. They didn't need anything from her in return to offer her a smile or a wave. They were simply showing kindness to another human being.

It was where she belonged. Where she had *always* belonged.

She could feel her eyes welling up with tears that she quickly blinked back, and when she glanced up at her friends, she saw that they had both stiffened in their chairs, their gazes locked on each other. They seemed to be communicating silently with each other about something important, though for the life of her, Tana had no idea what.

"No. *No.* Do *not* give him the satisfaction of seeing you cry," Selene said in a fierce whisper when she turned and caught sight of Tana's face.

"Sorry, don't... what?" Tana gave her a bewildered look, and then followed Selene's line of sight toward the front of the restaurant.

Her heart stalled briefly at the sight of Derek, looking effortlessly handsome in the gray blazer she'd given him on his last birthday, his arm tucked around Lucia's waist. The Italian actress was impossibly beautiful in a strapless teal dress, her dark hair tumbling down her back in soft curls as she leaned into Tana's husband, her full lips curved in a smile as she spoke to a very nervous-looking Giancarlo. The host kept sliding glances their way, obviously unsure what to do, but Tana merely shook her head and turned back to her friends.

"So," she said, picking up her menu and perusing the entrees. "What do you think I should order tonight? I can't decide between the shrimp scampi or the spaghetti Bolognese." She scrunched up her nose in thought, then glanced up to find Daphne and Selene gaping at her. "What?" she asked.

Then she flicked her eyes toward the front of the restaurant. Even though she had been momentarily thrown by the sight of Derek, once the initial flash of shock had subsided, she realized that she no longer cared. Let him eat wherever he wanted; it was a free country. Tana was going to enjoy her evening, and then, in a few days, she was going to hop a plane back to Dolphin Bay.

Back to Reed.

Back to where she belonged.

"I WISH I HAD YOUR STRENGTH," Daphne said, yawning widely as she opened the tube of toothpaste from her suitcase and squirted some onto her toothbrush. "If I were in your position, I would have marched over to their table and wrung their necks. But you just ate your dinner as if he wasn't sitting twenty feet away with, with… *her*," she finally settled on, her voice caustic. She shook her head and raised the toothbrush to her lips. "Honestly, Tana, I don't know how you do it."

"I don't know that it's strength," Tana said, slipping her feet into a pair of fuzzy socks and wiggling her toes for good measure. She pressed her hand to her stomach and groaned; the spaghetti Bolognese had been followed by an enormous piece of tiramisu—on the house, courtesy of an awkward Giancarlo who seemed to be doing his best to avoid a showdown in the middle of the restaurant between the exes—and then a platter of freshly baked Italian cookies. And since

Selene was buying, there was wine too. Lots and lots of wine.

"I think it's more that I'm just... done. I can't spend any more time crying over that man. I'm ready to move on with my life. I think..." Tana hesitated, unsure if she should voice her feelings out loud for the first time. *To heck with it*, she thought, then finished, "I think I'm ready to date again. I'm not getting any younger, and if the right man is out there, why should I wait another second?"

"That's the spirit," Daphne said, rinsing her teeth and sliding her toothbrush back into its holder. "And it *is* strength, Tana—I recognize that, even if you don't." She pulled her friend into a hug. "Thank you for a wonderful day, and a delicious dinner. I can't believe I left Maine only this morning—it's been a whirlwind day, and I'm beat. If it's okay with you, I'm going to hit the sack."

"Of course. And thank you again for coming to visit—you don't know what it means to me to have your support."

The two women said goodnight and padded off to their respective bedrooms, Daphne still yawning widely, barely able to keep her eyes open. Tana was exhausted too, but she wasn't ready to go to bed just yet. She had something much more important to attend to first.

She pulled out her laptop and set it on the bed, then climbed in beside it, propped herself against the pillows, and tucked the blanket around her legs. When she was comfortable, she opened the laptop, then grabbed her phone from the nightstand and listened once more to Uncle Henry's message before typing "Penelope Yeats" into the search engine.

Leaning her head against the pillow and releasing a long sigh, she closed her eyes and waited for the page to populate, hoping that the search for Penny would be a simple one but knowing that was probably unrealistic.

Then she opened her eyes and stared at the screen. Over one million hits. Fantastic.

She had a feeling it was going to be a long night.

Link by link, Tana waded through the first ten pages of search results. Most were irrelevant, where only the first or last name was a match—or sometimes neither, which had Tana shaking her head in frustration—but finally, on the eleventh page, she hit on something that looked promising. It was a link to an old, photocopied page of what appeared to be a women's publication from the early 1960s called *New York Lady*. The article was titled "Best New Carpet Cleaners to Keep Your Home Sparkling," written by a Penelope Yeats. It had to be a match.

Tana rolled her eyes as she scanned the article,

noting with irritation how women of that time period were expected to be good little homemakers —the writer was almost feverish with excitement about a product called Old Pine Spot Remover, or was at the very least excellent at pretending to be. She finished reading the article and searched for another, this time typing the magazine's name into the search engine alongside "Penelope Yeats."

A few more articles popped up, with more of the same headings, and then no additional matches were found. Tana tried keying in a few more combinations, but no dice. Penny seemed to have disappeared off the face of the earth. Navigating back to the search engine, Tana typed the name of the magazine, seeing with a sinking feeling of disappointment that the publication had been out of print since 1972.

Then she clicked to the next page of search results and her heart shot up into her throat—there in front of her was the list of editors who had worked for the magazine right before it folded. This was the best lead she'd found yet, so Tana quickly jotted down the news editor's name and opened up a new tab, keying in "Martha Lyle."

Another million search results, although this time, Tana struck gold. It turned out that Martha Lyle had a long and successful career in the publishing industry, beginning with *New York Lady* and ending as the editor-in-chief of a popular national women's magazine called *American Woman* that Tana herself had read plenty of times. A few quick clicks told Tana that Martha had retired from the magazine only six years prior; the grand party the publication had thrown for her exit even got a mention in *People*.

Tana glanced at the clock automatically, though she knew it was far too late for the offices of *American Woman* to be open. "Tomorrow," she promised herself, and Uncle Henry too, even though he was three thousand miles away and probably already asleep. Then she closed her laptop and turned off the bedside light, her thoughts on Penny until she finally drifted off to sleep.

CHAPTER 10

*S*ummer 1957

The sun was setting in a coral sky as Henry approached the bench at the end of the boardwalk, his steps heavy and halting. It was more crowded than the last time he and Penny had met here, the summer tourist season now in full swing. Weaving through the groups of people laughing, chatting, and watching the last rays of the sun dip below the horizon before they headed back to their hotels for the evening, Henry kept his eyes on the boardwalk's worn wooden planks. He was exhausted, and even the short walk to meet Penny here, at their spot, felt like an enormous undertaking.

Grief could do that to a person, he supposed.

Make every step feel like a marathon, every breath like a dying man gasping for air.

"Henry."

Mick, a boy he had grown up with who would soon be leaving the island for the state university, stopped Henry with a hand on his shoulder. Henry looked up reluctantly, not wanting his old friend to see his red-rimmed eyes. But when Henry met his gaze, Mick's eyes were warm with sympathy. "I'm so sorry about your father. He was a good man, and he'll be sorely missed."

"Thank you." The words were automatic, constantly on the tip of his tongue over the past two days. The hours since his father's death had been a blur, filled with funeral arrangements and choosing a headstone for the cemetery that looked out over the blue waters surrounding the island. It was the most peaceful resting place anyone could ask for, but Henry couldn't imagine leaving his father there for all eternity.

And then there was his mother—to say she was grief-stricken would be a grand understatement. Since his father had taken his last breath, she had been curled up in the room they'd shared at the inn, lying motionless under the covers, refusing to eat or drink or do anything but mourn the man she'd spent most of her life with.

Even in his own grief, Henry had to take over the running of the inn in her absence, because guests had been booked for months and bills needed to be paid. He did his best to keep up a sunny outward appearance, not wanting to clue them in on what was happening behind the scenes, but the effort drained every last ounce of energy from him, leaving him feeling exhausted.

Mick clasped Henry's hands and said goodbye before Henry continued trudging toward the bench, his stomach working its way into an even bigger knot as he spotted Penny waiting for him, chewing on the end of her long blonde ponytail, the way she always did when she was anxious. She had been a source of immeasurable comfort for him over the past two days, stopping by multiple times with casseroles, helping to check in the inn's guests and ensure they had what they needed for an enjoyable stay, and acting as a shoulder for Henry to lean on when things started to overwhelm him. Her actions since his father's death only highlighted for Henry how much he needed her, how he couldn't imagine a life without her.

And tonight, he was going to break her heart.

"Hey."

Penny's voice was soft as she jumped to her feet and held her arms out to Henry. He wanted to fall into her embrace, to breathe in the vanilla-and-lavender scent of her hair, but he stopped himself. He was no longer deserving of those things.

She looked slightly bewildered but did her best to hide it as he stepped around her outstretched arms and perched on the edge of the bench, his shoulders hunched. He could barely look at her, but he forced himself to meet her gaze anyway.

Penny hesitated for a moment before dropping onto the bench beside him, leaning into him, and whispering, "I love you." She reached for his hand, but he tugged it away; this time, the hurt on her face was achingly clear.

"Henry?" She paused, fingers flexing in her lap as if she was trying to figure out what to do with them. "Are you okay?" Then she winced. "That was a silly question, sorry. Of course you're not okay. But I mean, are you..." She trailed off, nibbling on her bottom lip, while Henry squeezed his hands into fists so tight that the knuckles turned white and began throbbing from the tension.

"Penny, I can't see you anymore."

He had to deliver the news before he couldn't bear to. He had to set her free so she could live her life without the burden he would represent. She would spread her wings and soar; he would tuck them into his sides and settle in right where he was.

Things were probably always meant to play out this way.

If Henry told himself that enough times, maybe he could convince himself it was true.

She reeled back on the bench, away from him, her eyes widening. "What?"

Henry stared at his clenched hands, his chest rising and falling rapidly as he tried to steady the rapid pounding of his heart. "I'm sorry. I just don't think it's a good idea."

Penny's beautiful blue eyes filled with tears, but she blinked furiously to banish them. When she spoke next, her voice was shaky as she fought to keep it under control. "Henry... please. I know you're devastated about what happened to your father, but that doesn't mean..."

She swallowed hard and shifted on the bench so that their legs were touching. "That doesn't mean anything about *us* has to change. You and me, we're... we're in love, aren't we?" The last words were spoken in a small, uncertain voice that was an arrow piercing Henry's chest, aimed directly for his heart.

He opened his mouth, trying to find the words he knew he needed to say to answer her question, but he faltered, a bitter taste on his tongue. Penny sniffled softly beside him as the seconds ticked by, but then her back stiffened and she reached over and pressed one finger under his chin, forcing him to look at her.

"This isn't about the inn, is it? Because Henry, I'll stay and help you get things sorted out. I can call the university, let them know that I need to postpone my enrollment." Her voice became stronger, more animated. "There's always next year, or even the year after! We'll help your mother until she's back on her feet, and then we can live the life we've always dreamed of. Your father would want that for you, Henry. He knows how much we mean to each other."

He did. He had. But Stephen Turner also had no idea that his only son had planned on leaving the island, possibly forever. If he had, would he have still asked Henry to take over the inn, to take care of his mother? Maybe, maybe not. The answer didn't matter anymore. His father's death had changed his life irreversibly, and no amount of love and longing he had for Penny could alter that.

He inhaled deeply, breathing in the salty ocean air like a lifeline. He wouldn't have Penny anymore, but he would always, *always*, have the island. And that counted for something. It also gave him the strength to forge on, to barrel his way through the worst conversation of his life.

"It's not the inn, Penny. It's you and me. I just... I don't love you anymore. I'm sorry."

Once the words were out, Henry felt something close to relief. The burden he had been carrying on his shoulders, the grief pressing down on his chest, had been almost too much to bear. But now the lie was out, and he could start to move on—in whatever way he could. Because even at the tender age of seventeen, when his entire life was stretched before him, abundant in its possibilities, Henry knew that these moments on the bench would shape him in ways he couldn't even begin to fathom.

Penny gasped. "You don't mean that." This time her voice was laced with anger. She prodded him in the chest with a surprisingly strong finger. "Henry Turner, you know as well as I do that that's a lie. You don't mean it."

"I do. I'm sorry." He gazed into her blue eyes, wet with unshed tears, and memorized the way the dying light highlighted the flecks of gold in her irises. It was the last time he would ever see her face, outside of his dreams.

She turned and fled from the bench, her footsteps pounding on the boardwalk's weathered planks as she ran toward town.

The next day, she left for New York City and a

future that was far brighter than the one he could have ever given her.

CHAPTER 11

"*N*o, she didn't work for *American Woman*. She was a writer for a magazine where Martha Lyle, your former editor, used to work. *New York Lady*. Have you ever heard of it?"

Tana bit back her annoyance as she clutched her cell phone in one hand while balancing her open computer on her lap. She'd relayed her story to no less than four people at *American Woman* magazine, and she still didn't seem to be getting anywhere.

"Let me put you on hold, hon, okay? I'll see if I can find someone who might be able to help."

"No, please, *please* don't put me on hold again. I—"

But soft music was already playing on the line, and Tana rapped her knuckles against her forehead in frustration. The next room over, she could hear

Daphne thumping around as she packed up another box of Tana's things to prepare to be shipped to Dolphin Bay. Tana felt guilty for not joining her, but Daphne had insisted that finding Penny was of the utmost importance and that she could handle a few minutes of packing on her own while Tana made the call.

Unfortunately, those few minutes were quickly turning into an hour, and Tana was no closer to finding Penny than she had been before she'd ever even heard of her.

"Daphne? You okay in there?" she called when she heard a particularly loud thump followed by an "Owww."

"I'm fine," Daphne called back a moment later. "Just whacked my toe on a massive metal box of... baseball cards?" She sounded bewildered. "I didn't know you were such a fan."

Ah, yes. Another of Derek's expensive hobbies. Usually he kept the box of valuable cards under their own bed... Tana wondered if he was trying to hide them from her so she wouldn't go after them in the divorce. As if she had any use for them anyway.

Before she could call back to Daphne—and resisting the urge to tell her to dump them down the toilet—the line clicked twice and the music cut off abruptly. "Hello?" a woman said. "I hear you're looking for Martha Lyle? I'm sorry, but she no longer works for this publication. She's been retired for some time now."

Tana gazed at the ceiling, willing herself to be patient. She was, after all, calling them with a strange request. "Yes, I did read that Ms. Lyle had retired. I was actually calling to see if you could put me in touch with her. She used to work for a magazine called *New York Lady*..." Once again, Tana launched into her spiel, though she was starting to feel like she was wasting her breath.

This time, though, when she had finished telling the woman on the other end of the line about Henry and Penny, there was a long pause. When the woman spoke next, she sounded slightly emotional. "Wow, that's quite a story you have there... Tana, did you say? I would love to help your uncle—"

Tana's heart leapt with excitement.

"—but unfortunately, it's against policy for me to give out Martha's contact information."

And then it plummeted right back down again.

There was another long pause as the woman appeared to be considering Tana's predicament. Then she said, "You know what? Martha and I worked together for many years, and I have her personal contact information. I'll reach out to her and give her the rundown on what's happening, and she can contact you directly if she thinks she can help you."

"Thank you! Thank you so much." Tana could scarcely keep the emotion out of her voice as she pictured telling Uncle Henry that she had found Penny at last. This was the most promising lead she had yet... she just had to pray that it worked out.

"No problem, I'm happy to help," the woman said. "I'm actually in a lull between projects right now, so I'll give her a call when we hang up. Hopefully she'll have some information for you that will help your uncle find his lost love." She paused, and when she spoke next, Tana could tell that she was holding back tears. "I hear a lot of rough stories, working in the media. This one sounds beautiful, and I hope it has a happy ending."

"Me too," Tana said, her fingers tightening around the phone. "Me too."

After they hung up, Tana jotted a few notes into her laptop, then reviewed what little information she had about the elusive Penny for a few minutes before closing her computer and sliding off the bed. "Daph, how's it going in there?" she called, stopping in the doorway to find her friend holding a framed family photo of Tana, her mother Julie, and her brother Jax.

"Oh, wow, I haven't seen this one in years." Tana

stepped forward and gently removed the frame from Daphne's hands. As she did, she noticed that her friend had an odd look on her face, but before she could ask her about it, Tana's cell phone rang in the other room and she practically bounded toward the door.

She flung herself into the bedroom and made a wild grab for the phone, her heart thumping when she saw the unfamiliar number on the caller ID. There was no way that Martha Lyle could be calling her so quickly, was there?

"Hello?" she said breathlessly when she had accepted the call, her fingers slipping off the button in her excitement to answer it. "This is Tana Martin."

"Hello there, Tana, my name is Martha Lyle. I just received a call from a former colleague at *American Woman* who told me that you wished to speak with me about Penelope Yeats?" Martha's voice was strong and clear, with a hint of a Southern accent.

"Yes, thank you so much for getting back to me so quickly. Do you remember Penelope?" She held her breath, waiting for the disappointing news that Martha held no memory of the pretty young woman her uncle had fallen for all those years ago.

"I absolutely do. Penny was one of my dearest friends back in the day. We were two of only a few women in the publishing industry at that time, and so we bonded over our shared struggles trying to make it in a man's world. She was tenacious, and vivacious, and an all-around lovely person. We only worked at *New York Lady* together for a short time before she left to pursue a career in newspaper. I stayed on at the magazine and rose to the position of news editor before it folded, but we kept in touch while I was there."

"Have you spoken to Penny recently? Do you know where I could find her? How I could talk to her?" The questions were tumbling out of Tana's mouth faster than she could think of them, her fingers flying across her laptop keyboard as she made note of everything Martha said.

Martha sighed. "Sadly, no. The last time I saw Penny was on her wedding day—I was one of the guests at her reception. She moved to… let me think for a moment, it's been so many years." Martha clucked her tongue over the line while Tana tried to keep her devastation in check. She had been *so close*. "Wisconsin, I think it was? Her new husband was offered a job there, something in accounting, I can't remember for sure. It's been close to fifty years." She whistled, low and long, and Tana could imagine the old woman shaking her head. "Could it really have been that long since I last saw Penny? My, the years do fly by, don't they."

Tana leaned back against the pillow on her bed, releasing a sigh of her own. Not only was fifty years a long time to have been out of touch with someone, but finding out that Penny was married threw an entirely new wrench in Tana's plans to reunite her and Uncle Henry. Why she hadn't considered that possibility was beyond her—of course Penny had gotten married in the years since she'd left Dolphin Bay. Most women of that era were quick to settle down and start a family.

"Well, Martha, thank you so much for your help," Tana said, closing her laptop once more. "I appreciate you taking the time to call me—"

"Hold your horses." The woman's Southern accent grew thicker as she let out a laugh. "I wouldn't have called you up just to tell you I haven't spoken to Penny in fifty years, would I? While I don't have any contact information—or any idea where in the world she could be, really—I do remember her husband's last name, and I thought that might help you in your search. It was Arbuckle. Gordon Arbuckle. He went by Gordy. Oh, he was a catch, that man. Tall, dark, and handsome, with these piercing blue eyes. I was so jealous of Penny on their wedding day—that's one of the reasons I remember his name after all these years."

She laughed lightly. "And Penny was radiant—she

never looked so beautiful or so happy in all the time I'd known her. They were a golden couple."

Tana winced at that—Giancarlo, the host at Bella Sera, had used those words about her and Derek just last night. And while she was happy to hear that Penny had found a husband, none of this information boded well for Uncle Henry. The image she had of reuniting him with Penny after all these years was quickly being replaced by one of the old man sitting alone in his room at the inn, his cane by his side, his good hand clutching the photos he'd kept tucked away for six decades. She could hardly bear it, but still, she had to ask…

"Did she ever mention anyone by the name of Henry Turner? Penny, that is."

Martha paused, and Tana could tell by the silence over the line that she was casting her mind back over the years, trying to remember a forgotten conversation between two long-ago girlfriends trying to make a name for themselves in the big city.

"No, dear, I'm afraid I can't remember anything of the sort. That doesn't mean it didn't happen, of course—a lifetime has passed since Penny and I used to gossip in the hallways of *New York Lady*. But I can't recall her mentioning any man other than Gordy—the two of them met at college and dated for years before tying the knot."

Then she added gently, "I'm sorry. I know that's not what you had wanted to hear from me, but I do hope that giving you her last name will allow you to track her down and finally give your uncle some kind of closure. We all deserve that in our lives, don't we?"

"We do," Tana murmured, thinking back to her encounter with Derek at the house just two nights ago, when he had said goodbye to her before leaving with Lucia. It was the end of their love story, the final page in their book. Her uncle didn't have that yet—and she desperately wanted to help him write it, one way or another.

Amid the distant sound of Tana speaking on the phone in the next room, Daphne sat on the ground, her eyes on the framed photo of Tana's family. It was taken years ago, when Tana and her brother Jax were still teenagers—and despite the two decades that had passed, Tana still looked much the same as the girl Daphne grew up with on Dolphin Bay, with her long brown hair and wide brown eyes that sparkled with life and laughter. That laughter may have dimmed a little lately, but Daphne knew it would be back again—helped along, of course, by

Reed. Those two were meant for each other. They just didn't know it yet.

That last thought brought a heaviness to Daphne's heart that she tried unsuccessfully to will away. Her fingertips automatically traced the lines of Jax's face, lingering on his mischievous grin. How many times he'd turned that grin on Daphne, his dark eyes glimmering with mirth, she had no idea— but she did know that when she was a girl, she lived for those moments.

She and Tana had been the best of friends during the summer months, and every year, Daphne looked forward to the day when she would see her friend stepping off the island's ferry, her suitcase packed with swimsuits and suntan lotion and books and all the other things that were required for a relaxing summer spent at the beach. They would squeal and jump into each other's arms, eager to spend the next three months playing in the surf and biking on the island's dirt paths and eating ice cream cones on the boardwalk, their feet dangling high above the water.

Yes, she loved Tana.

But she had been *in* love with Jax.

She could picture it now as though it were yesterday—she and Jax walking along the island's sandy shoreline as the setting sun cast coral rays across the sky, their hands entwined, their steps in sync. They had met when Daphne was only ten years old, but from the moment she laid eyes on him, she knew he was the one for her. It had taken him seven more years to acknowledge that he felt the same way, and when he whispered that to her as they sat on the sand with his head in her lap, she thought her heart would burst from happiness.

She'd made plans for the future.

He'd broken them.

She'd spent years trying to forget. It was easier now that Jax and Tana were no longer summer residents of the island. And then Tana had burst back into her life without warning, and with that came the memories of the boy she'd done her best to squash as the months turned into years, and the years turned into two decades since she'd seen his face.

She would have been happy to never see his face again.

Quietly, she turned the photograph over and resumed packing up Tana's things.

CHAPTER 12

*L*uke Showalter heard the familiar thumping of the old man's cane against the ground and squeezed his eyes shut, inhaling and exhaling a long, deep, calming breath. *He's just nervous*, he reminded himself for the hundredth time that day alone. Luke had spent forty years on the island, his parents moving to Dolphin Bay to open up an art gallery when he was in kindergarten. And even then, when he could barely hold a crayon straight, he knew to stay away from Old Man Turner, the island's resident grouch.

Never in his wildest dreams did he think he would someday be renovating Henry's beloved inn, working with the man on a much-too-close basis for months on end.

Wait a minute. Luke frowned. Only two days had

passed since he and his crew started work on the inn. It only *felt* like months.

Nevertheless, he was happy that Reed had recommended him for the job. Reed was a relative newcomer to the island—if you could count twenty years as being a newcomer, which most of the islanders did—but when Luke had taken up ocean kayaking as a hobby, he had found a kayak buddy and friend in Reed. Right now, though, he was seriously considering wringing his neck. Maybe this had been Reed's idea of a colossal practical joke.

"There's dust everywhere," the old man said by way of greeting, thumping his cane to a stop a few feet away from Luke and glaring at him, his faded green eyes sharp with annoyance. "I can barely breathe; keep it up and I'm going to need an oxygen tank." He coughed, loud and long, and cleared his throat while staring pointedly at Luke.

The contractor glanced around the inn's foyer, then swept his finger along the scratched wood surface of the front desk. His fingertip came away clean. He did the same with the drapes, a faded, bedraggled bouquet of fake flowers in an old vase, and a miniature lighthouse figurine perched on a shelf. Clean, clean, and more clean, as he had expected. His crew was taking every precaution necessary to keep the disruptions at the inn to a minimum, like they did with every job. Luke took pride in his work. He never let safety precautions slide. The old man was just looking for trouble—in fact, he seemed to be in a worse mood than Luke had ever seen him.

And that was saying something.

"I apologize, sir," he said, biting his tongue to keep from letting his true feelings color his words. "I'll speak with my crew again and make sure all of our plastic coverings are in place, and of course, my offer from earlier still stands: if you'd like me to book you a room at another hotel or inn, either on the island or elsewhere, I'd be happy to, and I'll personally foot the bill."

With pleasure, he added privately to himself. Anything to keep Henry Turner out of his hair, if even for a day or two. The inn's renovations were going well so far, but they had scarcely begun—a job of this scope would take at least a couple of months, and that was with his best crew working practically around the clock. Luke was a friendly, easygoing kind of guy—or so he'd been told—but everyone had their limits. And so far, Henry had been doing his level best to test them to their max.

"I already told you, I'm not leaving my home," the old man growled, thumping his cane once on the worn hardwood floors for good measure. "So you'll just have to find a workaround." He turned around with some difficulty, given the limited mobility on his left side, and began limping back down the hall. As he walked away, a piece of paper that had been poking out of his pants pocket fluttered to the ground.

"Sir, you dropped something," Luke said, bending down to grab it. When he turned it over, he realized it wasn't a piece of paper after all, but an old photograph, worn at the edges from being handled many times over the years. A teenage girl smiled back at him from the photograph, her eyes full of laughter, a smattering of freckles strewn across her nose. She was holding out her hand, as though trying to reach the photographer, and Luke immediately recognized Dolphin Bay as the background, the old Ferris wheel that had been torn down a decade ago clearly visible in the distance.

Henry Turner was suddenly standing in front of him, his cane clattering to the ground as he swung out his good arm to swipe the photo back from Luke. He immediately lost his balance, good arm windmilling at his side, and he would have toppled right onto the ground at Luke's feet if Luke hadn't shot out an arm to steady him. He guided Henry to a nearby armchair and handed him his cane, then cast one more glance at the girl's smiling face before gently placing the photograph back in the old man's wrinkled hands.

"Old girlfriend?" he asked as Henry stared down at the photo, his eyes unfocused. Then the man snapped his face up to Luke's, as if prepared to issue another verbal retort, before he sighed heavily and shook his head.

"A ghost," he said, his normally clear voice sounding gravelly around its edges, as if he was trying to hold his emotions in check. "Of a life that was so long ago I can barely remember it."

"Ah." After a moment of hesitation, Luke dragged a matching armchair over to Henry's side and plopped into it, glad for a quick rest, even if his companion wasn't the easiest to engage in a conversation with. He glanced at the photo, which was now shaking in the older man's hands. "I have one of those too," he added quietly, his mind automatically traveling back to his wedding day. He and his ex-wife, Lydia, had been so happy then. So full of excitement for what the future would bring.

Unfortunately, it had brought nothing but sorrow and heartache. But that was a chapter of his life that Luke had closed long ago. No sense dredging up the past when there were plenty of things to occupy his time in the present. He kept busy for many reasons—and one of those reasons was definitely not so he could keep the memory of the day she left him at bay.

Definitely, definitely not.

Luke realized he had been staring at his hands, which were clenched in his lap. When he looked up, he saw that Henry was watching him carefully, his eyes looking even more faded than usual, as if some of the life had been stripped from them. "I'm not one for giving advice," he said, tucking the photograph into the pocket of his button-down shirt. "But let me say this to you."

The old man's eyes bored into Luke's.

"Don't let whatever haunted your past linger in your present and future. No good can come from dwelling on things you cannot change. Take it from someone who's spent a lifetime trying to forget."

And without another word, Henry heaved himself to his feet and began limping away, the thump-thump-thumping of his cane echoing down the hallway as Luke watched him go.

REED DAWES WHISTLED as he strode through Dolphin Bay's main square, waving and calling greetings to the familiar faces he passed along the way. It was a beautiful day on the island—the air was crisp and clean, the sun was brilliant in the cerulean sky, and the ocean was a stunning turquoise color that was so clear it looked unreal. And Reed had a bounce in his step, courtesy of the hours-long telephone conversation he'd had with Tana a couple nights ago. He couldn't remember feeling such a strong connection to someone he'd known for such a short time, and definitely no woman he'd ever dated.

Or not dated, as in Tana's case.

Still, his mother's words had been ringing in his ears ever since he hung up the phone, his adrenaline too high to even think of sleeping. Instead, he'd taken a moonlit stroll to the opposite side of the island, which featured a rocky, forested coastline and dramatic, sweeping views. It was much quieter there, even during tourist season—most visitors to Dolphin Bay preferred to soak up the sun on the golden-sand beaches, but Reed always preferred the solitude of the island's untamed eastern shores.

If you don't pursue her, if you don't see what this could lead to, then your heart will be broken just the same.

Would it? Truth be told, Reed had never had a broken heart—not the romantic kind, at least. He, along with the rest of his family, had been torn to shreds when his father passed away from cancer far too young, but he'd never cared for a woman enough to be heartbroken when the relationship ended.

He'd never been in love.

Was he now?

Tana's face filled his mind—those beautiful brown eyes that always held a hint of laughter, her full lips that smiled easily, the freckles that ran along her nose and cheeks, which were becoming more prominent the longer she spent on the island. He cared for her, more than he was probably admitting to himself. And he knew that if he let himself, he could fall for her.

But things were messy. Getting involved with a woman going through a divorce, a woman who was still trying to mend her own broken heart no matter how brave a face she put on every day, would be difficult, to say the least.

Still, couldn't the most difficult things in life also be the most rewarding? His father used to say something to that effect, but a teenaged Reed had always brushed him off. Now, he wished he hadn't. He could use some advice from a man who had experienced love, and loss, and all the things that came with aging, but his father was no longer here to guide him.

And that was a shame.

Reed pulled himself out of his thoughts as he turned up the inn's cobblestone sidewalk and headed for the front door. He was pleased to see his friend

Luke's crew hard at work on the inn's renovations, and he was even more pleased that Tana had chosen Luke as her contractor in the first place. The man was as solid as they came—he was dependable, hard-working, and had an incredible eye for detail and design. Reed had no doubt that under Luke's watchful eye, the inn would soon return to its former glory, and then some.

And speak of the devil...

"What are you doing here?" Luke asked, stepping out the front door as Reed approached the inn's expansive wraparound porch. Reed noticed that his friend's normally happy-go-lucky expression was gone, replaced with a hollow look that had Reed squinting at him in concern.

"You okay?" he asked, eyeing Luke up and down.

Luke flinched, but quickly covered the automatic reaction with his usual easygoing smile. "Never better," he said. He ran a hand through his blond hair and shook his head. "Just had a conversation with Henry, that's all. The man can be a little... intense."

"I'll say." Reed laughed. "Deep down, everyone on the island is a little afraid of him. Except my mother, that is. But you know how she is—she can even see the good in a mosquito biting her on the arm. She might even offer it one of her homemade casseroles once it was finished doing its business."

"Ah, too bad we can't all be like Edie. Life would be much easier." Luke eyed the paper bag in Reed's hand. "Don't tell me you got a burger from Sal's and came here to taunt me with it. You know I have a weakness for anything fried, greasy, and smothered in cheese."

"I know." Reed grinned and swung the bag back and forth. "That's why I brought two. I decided to take a long lunch and thought you might need a break yourself. I know how difficult Henry can be."

"Yeah, especially since you've been spending all your spare time at the inn lately." Luke bounded off the porch steps and joined Reed on the short walk to the beach, the two men brushing past the long dune grass that lined the winding dirt path that led down to the sandy shore. "And something tells me you aren't there to visit Henry." He gave Reed a sly look that Reed returned with a solemn one of his own.

"I'm not. That's where I'm hoping you come in. I need some advice, and I hope you don't mind letting me pick your brain for a little while."

"A burger that comes with strings attached." Luke shook his head playfully. "I should have known it was a trick."

The path widened as they approached the beach, and both men automatically bent down to slide off their shoes before stepping into the pillowy-soft sand. The beach was packed with vacationers, and colorful umbrellas, folding chairs, and coolers dotted the sand as far as the eye could see.

Both men took a few minutes to enjoy the scenery and breathe in deep lungfuls of the salty ocean air before making their way toward the shore, kicking up sand as they walked. They settled themselves on a short slope overlooking the water, and Reed unpacked two containers of hamburgers and fries before handing one to Luke, whose eyes were trained on a slender woman stretched out on a nearby towel, a book in her hand and a floppy hat shading her face.

"Why don't you go over and say hello?" Reed said, nudging his friend in the side before squirting ketchup on his burger and raising it to his lips. He took a massive bite while Luke shook his head emphatically.

"No thanks. I've had my fill of women for a long, *long* time."

Reed gave him a sympathetic look. The divorce had been hard on Luke, and as far as Reed was aware, he hadn't so much as taken anyone out on a date in the past five years, ever since Lydia had packed her bags and left the island for good. Luke hadn't talked about her much since then, and Reed largely avoided the subject. But right now, he needed some perspective, and Luke was the best man for the job.

"Speaking of Lydia…" he began, unsure how to launch into such a thorny conversation.

Luke, who had just been about to take a bite of his own burger, set it down and winced. "Were we?" he asked, his voice tight. "That's a surefire way to ruin lunch."

"Sorry." Reed grimaced. "I know she's the last person you want to think about right now, but…" He took a deep breath. "As you seem to be aware—and at this point, it seems the rest of the island is too— I'm interested in Tana. I've never been shy about asking a woman out on a date, but this time, things are different. Her situation is messy. And I don't know—"

"If it's a good idea getting involved with someone in the middle of a divorce?" Luke finished Reed's sentence before he could even fully formulate his thoughts. He toyed with the lettuce poking out from his hamburger bun before tearing off a piece and rolling it between his fingers.

"Normally I'd say no, definitely not. Things between Lydia and I were contentious—or maybe 'ugly' is a better word for it, I don't know. I needed time to get over what happened, and I'm sure in her own way, she did too. But something old Mr. Turner said got me thinking—how we shouldn't let our past ruin our present and future. That applies to Tana more than you, but I guess what I'm saying is…"

Luke gazed out over the ocean, watching a lone dolphin dipping in and out of the waves, before turning back to Reed. "Go for it, because life is too short to do anything but what makes us happy. Definitely, definitely go for it."

CHAPTER 13

"Hey, you almost ready to go?" Daphne appeared in Tana's bedroom doorway, her suitcase at her feet. "As much as I've enjoyed seeing California for the first time, I have to admit, I'm a little homesick. I guess I'll always be a small-town girl at heart."

"I'm starting to think I'm the same way." Tana smiled at her friend from her position bent over her open suitcase, where she was cramming whatever odds and ends from the house she could fit inside. It was going to cost a fortune to ship the rest of her belongings to Dolphin Bay, so even a few pounds added off the total weight would result in money she could use to put toward the inn's renovations.

She glanced at the clock, then at her laptop,

which was sitting open on her bed. "I'll be down in a few minutes, okay?"

Daphne followed her gaze and gave her a knowing smile. "Okay. Just don't get so caught up in Henry and Penny's story that we miss our flight. Sal will have my head on one of the diner's platters if I miss my shift tomorrow. He already wasn't thrilled about letting me off these few days to begin with." Her eyes darkened and she shook her head. "I swear to you, me, and everyone on this earth that someday soon I'm going to leave that place for good."

"I know you will, and I promise I'll be there when you take off that waitressing apron for the last time." Tana grinned at her friend. "And I also promise that I won't make us miss our flight. Give me ten minutes and then we'll get going, okay?"

Even though she knew they'd be cutting it tight, especially given LA's infamous traffic, Tana was itching to continue the search for Penny. She and Daphne had been so busy finishing packing up the house that she hadn't had a chance to do any more research since her phone call with Martha Lyle.

She shut her suitcase and plopped down onto it, flattening it as much as she could as she struggled to pull the zipper all the way around. When she finally stuffed the last of the items inside and finished zipping it, she made a beeline for her computer, keying in the password and immediately pulling up the search engine. She typed "Penelope Arbuckle" and hit the enter key, waiting for the results with bated breath.

Nothing of relevancy immediately caught her eye, so with another glance at the clock, she navigated to an online people directory and typed Penelope's married name into the search bar.

Bingo. Only two results, both women approximately the correct age. The first Penelope Arbuckle lived in Santa Fe, New Mexico, and the other in a tiny town called Stowe, Vermont. When the website wouldn't let her proceed any further without payment, Tana heaved a sigh and dug around in her purse for her wallet, sliding out her credit card and keying in the numbers. By the time she finished typing in all of her information, Daphne was calling out from downstairs, her voice edged with panic, "Tana, come on, we're going to miss the flight!"

"Coming," Tana called back, then quickly jotted down each woman's phone number before snapping her laptop shut and grabbing her purse. As she hurried down the stairs, she could scarcely keep the grin off her face from the feeling of excitement that was stirring inside her.

Uncle Henry was finally going to have answers. And he was going to have them soon.

~

"I'M ALL for a good love story, but I don't understand why you just can't wait a few hours until we're home. Shouldn't you at least try to eat something before we board the plane? It's going to be a long flight."

Daphne waved her ham and cheese sandwich in Tana's direction, but she merely shook her head, her fingers fumbling for her cell phone. Truth be told, she needed the distraction—anything to help Tana forget that she was leaving California, and her old life with Derek, behind for good.

"Suit yourself." Daphne shrugged and balled up her sandwich wrapper before turning to the massive iced cinnamon bun she'd bought. "If you need any help, let me know. Otherwise I'll be tucking into this little beauty." She tore off a piece of the cinnamon bun, popped it into her mouth, and moaned with delight, then waved goodbye to Tana as she made her way to a more secluded row of chairs.

She plopped into the nearest one, then scrolled through her phone's contact list until she came to the two new entries, both for Penelope Arbuckle. Figuring that the woman living in Vermont more likely to be Uncle Henry's Penny, she dialed that number first, her heartbeat quickening as the phone began to ring.

The call was just about to click over to voicemail when the ringing stopped and a thumping sound came over the line, as though someone was fumbling with the receiver. "Hello?" a distant voice said, and then, more clearly, "Hello? Who is this?"

Tana took a deep breath. "Hi, Mrs. Arbuckle? You don't know me, but my name is Tana Martin and I—"

"Betty, is that you? I told you I couldn't make it for lunch today, Sara is running a fever and I have to pick her up from the elementary school…"

"No, Mrs. Arbuckle, not Betty. This is Tana Martin and—"

"Lana who?"

"Tana Martin."

"Sorry, dear, we don't want any encyclopedias today. My husband already bought one set from you and I simply don't think we can afford another—"

There was a whispering sound on the other end of the line, followed by more fumbling, until another woman, sounding younger than the first, said, "Hello, this is Marie Quint. Can I help you?"

By now Tana was debating hanging up the phone, but she decided to forge on. "Hi, my name is Tana Martin, and I'm afraid you don't know me…

I'm looking for a woman named Penelope Arbuckle, and I hope this is the right number."

"It is." The second woman sounded cautious. "I'm Penelope's nurse. How can I help you?"

"This might sound a little strange, but I'm helping my uncle, a man named Henry Turner, track down a woman he used to know many years ago in the hopes that they can be reunited. Do you know if Penelope lived on the island of Dolphin Bay, off the coast of Maine, in the late 1950s? Did she then go on to be a journalist in New York?"

The woman sighed. "I'm sorry, Ms. Martin, but I'm afraid I can't help you with any of that. Mrs. Arbuckle has middle-stage Alzheimer's, and I was hired by her family only a few months ago to help care for her, so I don't know much about her personal history other than the little bit she's told me here and there. But she gets confused often, as you can imagine, and so it's hard for me to say if even what she's told me is true." She paused. "Her daughter lives in North Carolina, I believe, and if you'd like, I can try reaching out to her to see if she can help you…?"

Her voice trailed off, and in the background, Tana heard the older woman say, "Is that Betty? Tell her I can't come to lunch today. I already *told* her, I have to get Sara before—"

"No, Mrs. Arbuckle, it's not Betty," Marie said in a soothing voice as the woman started getting agitated. "Why don't you sit down on the sofa and I'll bring you a nice cup of tea, okay? And then we'll watch one of your programs. I think *The Price is Right* is going to be on soon." Then she returned to the line. "Sorry, what was I saying? Things are a little hectic around here today…"

"It's okay," Tana said, white-knuckling the phone. "You sound like you have your hands full, and I'm sorry to bother you. Have a nice day, okay? And thank you."

Then she hung up, staring at the phone for a few moments as she collected her thoughts. There was no need to bother Mrs. Arbuckle's daughter. Even if this was Henry's long-lost love, she would most likely have no memory of their time together, and Tana feared that would lead to even further heartbreak for her uncle. So with a heavy heart, she deleted the woman's information from her contact list and moved on to the next number, the Penelope Arbuckle who lived in New Mexico.

Steeling herself for more bad news, she tapped the call button, wincing as she waited for the phone to ring. This time, a woman picked up midway through the second ring—and Tana was relieved to hear that her voice sounded clear and friendly when she answered with a chipper, "Hello?"

"Hi," Tana said uncertainly, then cleared her throat and spoke in a stronger voice. "Hi, is this Penelope Arbuckle?"

"Penelope?" The woman laughed softly. "I suppose that's my name, yes, but I don't think I've gone by that since the day I was born, and trust me, that was a long time ago. The name's Penny, dear. Do I know you?"

Tana's breath stalled. This was it. This was Penny. She knew it as certainly as she knew her own name.

"You don't know me, no... My name is Tana Martin, and I may be related to someone from your past."

Penny whistled. "Now you've got me intrigued. The last name Martin doesn't ring a bell, but like I said, I've been around since we had fewer than fifty states and my memory isn't as sharp as it used to be. What's your relative's name?"

By now, Tana's nerves had sharpened almost to the breaking point. "Henry Turner," she said, squeezing her eyes shut as she waited for the response. Somewhere along the way, Henry's quest to find Penny had become her own, and she had thrown herself into their story wholeheartedly. If it ended in disappointment for Uncle Henry… well, she wasn't sure she'd be able to handle that.

There was a sharp intake of breath, followed by such an extended period of silence that at first Tana wasn't certain that Penny was still on the line. But then she said, so softly that Tana had to strain to hear her, "Henry Turner? Now that's a name I haven't heard in over sixty years." Then she added, to herself, "Can it have been that long?"

Tana's eyes immediately welled with tears as she pictured the girl in the photos, fresh-faced and pretty, her eyes sparkling with life and youthfulness. "So your maiden name was Penny Yeats, and you used to live on Dolphin Bay Island? Now you're married to a man named Gordon Arbuckle?"

"The very same. Although Gordy, my husband, passed on many years ago." The woman paused again. "Is Henry… Are you calling because…?"

"Henry's alive and well," Tana hastened to say, picking up on the woman's unspoken words. "I'm calling because he asked me to find you."

"Wow." The woman laughed, although Tana thought the sound held a hint of sadness. "I think I might need to sit down for this." She inhaled again, and Tana could hear her blowing out a long breath. "I think you might also need to back up a little too, because I haven't seen hide nor hair of Henry Turner since the night he broke my heart. Why now, after all these years, does he want to find me?"

Broke *her* heart? Tana's jaw dropped. She'd always assumed the opposite was true, that Penny had left her uncle mourning the loss of whatever they'd once shared. Why else would he have kept those photos tucked away for so many years?

"Hello? Anyone there?"

Tana collected her thoughts and managed to rein in her surprise enough to say, "I don't know exactly why my uncle wants to find you, but he's been very determined." She paused. "I guess, like you said, I should back up a little, start at the beginning of the story. My uncle recently had a stroke, and I've been helping him run his inn on Dolphin Bay during his recovery. When I was looking through his records, I found an old photo of you, and when I brought it up to him, he mentioned that he'd like to speak with you again."

That was far from the whole truth, of course, but Tana didn't feel comfortable sharing that Uncle Henry had kept a bundle of photos of Penny tied up with a fraying red ribbon, or that he had been a basket case—even more so than usual—ever since Tana had unearthed them. Those details were private to her uncle, and if he wanted to delve into them with Penny, that was his business.

Which, of course, brought up the most pressing problem.

"He wants to see you, but the stroke left him with some mobility issues, and I just don't think it's possible for him to travel all the way to New Mexico." Tana cast her eyes around the bustling airport as she spoke, trying to imagine the stubborn old man navigating it with his cane. "Maybe…" She tapped her chin in thought. "Maybe we can schedule a video call over the computer one of these days?"

Even as she made the suggestion, though, she knew it wasn't enough—whatever closure Uncle Henry was seeking wouldn't be found through a virtual chat. He needed to sit down with Penny, and he needed to do it before any more health problems developed. Tana wanted whatever years were left in Henry's life to be spent at peace, and she sensed that couldn't happen until he reunited with the girl from long ago.

Penny was silent for another long moment, as if she was still trying to absorb everything that Tana had said. As she waited, Tana imagined what it must feel like for the woman to receive this call out of the blue. Somewhere down the road, when Lucia had undoubtedly tired of him, would Derek pick up the phone and try to make amends with Tana, the woman who had stood by him for twenty years before he broke her heart? And would she even want to hear him out?

As she thought about Derek, an image of Reed popped into her mind—of his effortless smile, his easygoing laugh, his kind eyes that crinkled at the edges. A knot of anticipation formed in her stomach, and she was struck with a sudden thought—she wasn't anxious about leaving California for the last time, as she'd believed, but nervous about seeing Reed again. Even though they hadn't spoken since, the conversation they'd had into the wee hours of the morning a few nights ago had changed them somehow, had wormed its way under the façade of their friendship to what was really lurking underneath—genuine feelings. From her and, she suspected, from Reed as well.

At least she very much hoped so.

When Penny spoke again, her voice was cautious. "I'll tell you what. I'm going to be flying back to Maine to visit my sister in two weeks—fortuitous timing, don't you think? Anyway, my parents moved off of the island not long after I went to college, and between that and, well, what happened with Henry…" She cleared her throat. "I never went back. But I loved that place, and it's high time I stepped foot on the island's beautiful shores again. So if it works for you—or Henry, I suppose—then I'll pop over to the inn and we can have a chat."

"That sounds perfect." Tana exhaled in relief. "The inn's address is—"

"Oh, honey." Penny interrupted her with a chuckle. "I know that island like the back of my hand. You and Henry pick the time, and I'll be there." She grew silent again. "And Tana?"

From the gate, Daphne began waving frantically to her, and Tana realized that her flight was starting to board. "Yes?" she said as she hitched her purse over her shoulder and rose from her seat.

"Tell Henry that I'm very much looking forward to seeing him."

CHAPTER 14

$\mathcal{T}$ana worked hard to conceal her disappointment when she and Daphne arrived at baggage claim and no one was there to greet them other than their fellow plane passengers and a carousel of suitcases. The entire flight home, she'd been picturing Reed waiting for her with a bouquet of red roses and a declaration of true love, as if she were a character in a romcom movie.

This whole Henry and Penny story must be getting in my head, she thought, falling into step beside Daphne, who, thankfully, was too busy looking for her suitcase to notice Tana's slightly crestfallen expression. Reed had been planning to meet Tana at the airport, but before Daphne had left the island, she'd told Reed not to bother—that she would accompany Tana back to Dolphin Bay herself.

Not that Tana wasn't grateful for a little more girl time. She and Daphne had a blast in Los Angeles, and her friend's presence had made a world of difference in soothing the sting of Tana's last few days in the house she and Derek had lovingly selected together, planning to grow old in it. She and Selene had parted ways that morning with a tearful hug and promises to meet up again soon, though Tana knew she wouldn't be making the trip to California anytime soon, and Selene's work as a busy realtor in one of the country's hottest housing markets left her with few opportunities for taking a true vacation.

"You ready to go?" Daphne said, wheeling her suitcase up to Tana. She grabbed her own, and the two women headed out of the airport to catch a taxi, and from there, to take the ferry back to Dolphin Bay. After the unending plane ride from California, Tana was exhausted just thinking about any more travel. But she was eager to return to the island, especially now that she had good news about Penny.

Although she had no idea how her uncle would take it.

Shrugging off that thought—a problem for later, she decided—Tana and Daphne made their way to the airport's taxi stand and took their place at the back of the short line. Daphne closed her eyes and leaned against the wall, her face lined with exhaustion, and Tana was just about to do the same when she felt her phone buzzing in her purse. Digging it out, she saw with surprise that her brother Jax was calling, and quickly answered the phone.

"Hey, Jax! Long time no talk."

Jax was only a year and a half older than Tana, and the two of them had always been close—but, like most relationships, the distance had driven a wedge between them, and they usually only made time for quick calls on holidays and birthdays. Now that she was back to living on the East Coast, she hoped to rekindle the close relationship they once had, although Jax's job as the head chef and owner of a popular restaurant in Philadelphia didn't give him the chance for much down time.

At the sound of Jax's name, Daphne's eyes had flown open and she was watching Tana with an expression that looked almost... wary? That couldn't be true—growing up, Daphne and Jax had spent almost as much time together during the summer as the two of them had, and Tana couldn't recall them not getting along, typical teenage spats about what to do on a Friday night aside, of course.

She frowned at Daphne and mouthed, *It's my*

brother, before returning her attention to the call. When she happened to glance back up, she saw that her friend now wore a slightly manic grin that Tana chalked up to the long day and stress of traveling.

"Hey, Tana, how's Uncle Henry doing?"

Jax sounded exhausted, unlike his usual gregarious self. Of the two of them, Jax had been the more outgoing one, always surrounded by a group of friends and getting into all kinds of mischief, most of it harmless. But Tana supposed that owning a restaurant was no small amount of work; it made her tired just thinking of the long days and nights he spent planning menus and cooking, not to mention running the business end of things.

"He's doing as well as can be expected," Tana said, balancing the phone on her shoulder as she and Daphne moved up in the line. "His arm and leg are already showing some improvement thanks to the physical therapy, but the doctors tell me it's going to be a slow process."

"I'm so sorry I haven't been there to help," Jax said. "What you're doing for Uncle Henry is amazing, and Mom told me all about the renovations to the inn. I feel terrible that you're handling this all alone…"

"Don't worry about it," Tana said, and meant it. "This has been a good thing for me. You know, a distraction from everything that's been happening in my life. But you should visit if you get the chance. I'm sure Uncle Henry would love to see you, and you'll never guess who I ran into my very first week on the island." She grinned at Daphne, whose smile had stretched, if possible, even wider. "Daphne! She's actually here with me right now. You remember her, right?"

There was a pause. "I do," Jax finally said, his voice oddly strained. "Tell her I said hey, okay? But I have to go now. I'll try to call you soon."

"Okay, bye—" Tana started to say, then pulled the phone away from her ear and frowned at it when she realized her brother had already hung up.

Daphne, who had been listening to their exchange, glanced at the phone as Tana slipped it back into her purse. "Jax doing okay?"

"He's fine," Tana said. "A little distracted, it seems, but we didn't get into it. Oh, look!" she added, pointing to the curb. It was finally their turn at the front of the line, and their taxi had chosen that moment to pull up.

Daphne looked relieved as they loaded their suitcases into the trunk and piled into the backseat, and as soon as she gave the driver directions to the nearest harbor where they would catch the ferry, she immediately leaned her head against the seatback. "If you don't mind, I'm going to try to take a nap on the way—I'm beat," she said, and then closed her eyes.

Tana studied her friend's face for a moment, then turned and gazed out the window as the taxi pulled away from the curb and navigated into traffic, the Maine sky a crystal blue on this beautiful summer day.

It was good to be home.

THE POUNDING of nails and grunts of the men working on the inn were audible as Tana pulled into the inn's gravel parking lot and stepped out of the golf cart she and Daphne had procured at the harbor after the ferry deposited them back on the island. She breathed in deeply, enjoying the fresh, salty ocean air, a far cry from Southern California's smoggy highways and bumper-to-bumper traffic. She'd expected to feel a deep sorrow upon leaving Los Angeles for what might very well be the last time, but instead, her soul felt lighter than it had in years.

And that lightness immediately turned to elation as the inn's front door opened and Reed stepped out, his hands shoved deep in the pockets of his jeans, a pair of sunglasses pushed onto his head. Their eyes locked and a grin spread across his face, and as he stepped onto the inn's wraparound porch, Tana hurried up to greet him.

She hesitated for a moment as she stood in front of him, unsure what to do but keenly aware that in her absence, something had changed between them. An electricity filled the air around them, an almost tangible excitement and the promise of things to come. Very good things, she hoped.

"Hey, you." He gave her that easy smile that always made her feel slightly off-kilter, and then he bridged the distance between them, bent down, and pulled her into his arms. "I missed you."

The embrace caught Tana off guard, and from the corner of her eye, she could see Daphne watching them from the golf cart, grinning at her and shooting her a thumbs-up before turning to unload Tana's bag from the back.

Tana took a deep breath, inhaling his vanilla-and-musk scent, and closed her eyes as she leaned her head against his shoulder. "I missed you too," she said when she finally pulled back, gazing up into his pale-blue eyes that were trained on hers.

He studied her face for a long moment, his expression inscrutable, and he had just opened his mouth to say something when the front door banged open and the familiar thump-thump-thump of a cane greeted Tana's ears.

All thoughts of Reed were pushed to the background as Uncle Henry stared at her from the doorway, his faded green eyes sweeping over her, his expression guarded. Even though his face betrayed no hint of emotion, she could tell by the tension in his posture that her next words would be some of the most important ones in his life.

So without hesitation, she walked toward him, his eyes following her every movement until she stopped in front of him, rested a hand on his shoulder, and whispered, "I found her, Uncle Henry. I found Penny."

She could hear Reed's sharp intake of breath behind her as her uncle reeled back slightly, his good hand white-knuckling his cane, and Tana automatically reached out a hand to steady him. She expected him to bat her away, like he did every time someone offered him help, but instead, he dropped the cane and leaned against the doorway, raising his shaking hand to his mouth as Tana watched him fearfully, positive that he would fall.

But instead, he looked over her head in the direction of town, his eyes taking on a faraway quality as though he was envisioning a time that had slipped away from him, like sand through fingertips, like a boy who had seen his girl for the last time on an evening not so different than this one, when the ocean rose up to greet the shore and the moon danced across the sparkling water.

And then he bowed his head and began to cry.

CHAPTER 15

*J*ax Keller sat on a barstool and leaned his elbows against the granite counter-top, running his fingers through his light brown hair again and again until it stood on end. The restaurant was quiet around him, the clatter of forks and knives and the din of conversation giving way to a deep, unyielding silence that settled over him like a blanket, making breathing difficult.

He had poured everything he had into making the restaurant a success—blood, sweat, tears, and every last penny he earned above and beyond what it took to keep the place running. Heck, he couldn't even remember the last time he'd taken a full paycheck for himself. There'd been no other choice. What was he supposed to do? Tell his bartender

Shayna, a single mother with two kids still in diapers, that he couldn't keep her anymore? Or should he deliver the blow to Clint, who was working around the clock in the kitchen, trying to scrape together as much money as he could to pay for his wife, who'd recently been diagnosed with early-onset Alzheimer's disease, to try out that new, promising drug that the insurance company was refusing to cover?

Jax was a single guy with few responsibilities. He could handle the bank account that had been marching steadily toward zero for years.

Until suddenly, he couldn't. Mostly because he'd stuck his head in the sand as deep as he could get it, the same refrain playing in his mind on an endless loop of denial: *Things will turn around. Things will turn around.*

His gastropub, The Brewhouse, had been a smash hit when he'd opened it on Philadelphia's Avenue of the Arts, a stretch of the city known for its performing arts venues. Those first few, heady years, he'd barely been able to keep up with the demand, and he thrived on the thrill of reading the critics' reviews in the papers and hearing the diners remark to themselves that the food was out of this world. He took pride in the fact that he used only the best vendors, and meticulously planned out a new menu every season, spending days holed up in his home kitchen practicing each recipe until it reached perfection.

Jax was a solid chef. He knew that. But all the skills in the world couldn't help him when the business manager he hired, a drop-dead-gorgeous girl with a stunning smile and sparkling eyes that always seemed to be turned his way, decided to start dipping into the restaurant's pockets to line her own. She'd enchanted Jax along the way, leading him to believe that she cared for him, that they had a future together, and all the while she was slowly and methodically destroying the life he had worked so hard to build.

By the time he figured out what was happening, it was far too late. The Brewhouse couldn't be saved. And tonight, he was here to say goodbye.

He climbed off the barstool, feeling far older than his forty-four years, and gazed at the rows of shelves that had once been filled with fine wines and liquors but now stood empty, save for a dingy dishrag that someone had left behind. Then, with a deep breath, he steeled himself and turned to face the dining room—the bare booths, the empty tabletops, the silence so thick it was practically deafening. He could still hear the laughter and conversation echoing through the room, the ghosts of the people who had made this place what he had always wanted: a home.

Growing up, life with Julie Keller was difficult. His mother never seemed all that interested in, well… mothering, and so he and his younger sister Tana were left with relatives for long stretches while she traveled the world as a wildlife photographer. Eventually, she decided they weren't worth the trouble anymore, and he and Tana were shipped off to boarding school and, in the summers, to his uncle's inn on Dolphin Bay. Jax had loved the island, but to him, it represented yet another way that he was unwanted. A burden, to his mother and then his uncle, who was a gruff, unaffectionate man who seemed perpetually distracted.

So Jax spent as much time as he could outside the inn, exploring the island's untamed coasts, pedaling his bike along its winding dirt paths, sitting on an old, weathered bench at the far side of the board-walk long into the night, when the gulls' cries had quieted and the vacationers were sound asleep in their beds. In a turbulent childhood, it was one of the few times he ever found peace.

And he was still searching for that peace. Maybe someday he would find it.

Jax finished his last tour of the dining room, then bypassed the kitchen on the way to the restaurant's front door. He couldn't bring himself to step inside one last time—to see the gleaming fixtures and the pristine countertops and remember how he had felt that first day when he tied his apron around his waist and felt, for the first time, that he was finally making a life for himself that was his own. One that no one could ever take away from him.

With a sigh, Jax slipped the key from his pocket, turning the cold metal over in his palm and memorizing every notch and nick. Then he set it on the hostess station, shouldered open the door, and stepped out into the night.

He had lost everything, so he had no choice but to start fresh.

But that would mean returning to the island.

It would mean owning up to breaking her heart.

DAPHNE WAVED goodbye to the last customers, two older men who liked to sit in their regular booth at Sal's Diner long into the night, playing Rummy and discussing the Patriots' prospects for winning the Super Bowl. She slumped into a booth, letting her head fall back onto the worn red vinyl as a soft sigh escaped her lips. She was drained, physically and mentally, and was in desperate need of a good, long vacation from the diner. A permanent one.

Soon, she reminded herself, her thoughts drifting to the Inn at Dolphin Bay. When she and Tana had returned from Los Angeles, they stepped right into the middle of a construction site—Luke, as usual, had a tight hold of the reins, and he and his crew were already a week ahead of schedule. The sooner the inn could reopen to the public, the better—for Henry, for Tana, and definitely, *definitely*, for Daphne.

Tana kept a cautious tone whenever the two of them discussed their plans for having Daphne supply breakfast and other goodies to the inn's guests—and Daphne understood why. Her friend knew she wanted to leave the diner for good, and she didn't want to get Daphne's hopes up that the inn would be the start of her ticket out of there. "Reservations are going to start slow," Tana had warned. "It might take a while before we can afford to bring you on."

But Daphne had spent her entire life on the island, and she knew what the inn could be. What it had been, before Henry Turner could no longer keep up with it. The Inn at Dolphin Bay would rise again, and Daphne would rise right along with it.

That was the plan, at least.

"Daphne? You out there? Before you clock out, I need you to finish wiping down the last table and prep all the dishes and silverware for the morning rush."

She cringed at the sound of Sal's harsh voice, like gravel and glass being ground together to create the world's worst symphony. He was an okay boss, she supposed, and he ran a tight ship, which was why his diner had stood the test of time when other restaurants closed their doors long ago. Nothing got by Sal. He also didn't like to give an inch to anybody, up to and including his head waitress, the woman who had been working for him since she was sixteen years old and still daydreaming about what her life would become.

Daphne hadn't meant to stay stuck in the same place for so long. But there were bills to pay, and to be honest... she had always been a little afraid to spread her wings. What if she fell to the ground with a splat?

But things were about to change. She could feel it in her bones.

CHAPTER 16

"Thanks, guys. I'll see you in the morning. Have a nice night."

Tana waved as the last of Luke's crew trooped out the front door in the waning light, shouldering wooden boards and wiping sweat from their brows. They had been hard at work for two weeks now, working in shifts from sunrise to sunset, always under Luke's watchful eye. The inn was covered in plastic sheeting, and despite the crew's best efforts, dust sometimes lingered in the air and tickled her nose, making her feel a perpetual need to sneeze.

But Tana didn't mind in the least. That meant progress was happening, which was all she could ask for.

She slipped into her favorite rocking chair on the inn's porch, the one with the creaky legs and the worn cushion that melded perfectly to her body, and gazed out over the darkening water. Most of the vacationers had packed up their umbrellas and coolers for the day, but their presence remained in the footprints scattered in the sand and the seagulls still poking around for crumbs they'd left behind. Tana had been so busy over the past few weeks that she'd been unable to really take the time to unwind and enjoy the inn's breathtaking views of the ocean, the lighthouse, and the hazy outline of the mainland in the distance, outside of stolen moments like this one.

But tonight, she was unable to relax, her body practically twitching with nervous energy as she envisioned what tomorrow would bring. Uncle Henry felt it too, she knew—when the old man was stressed out or anxious, he took to his room, and she hadn't seen him since breakfast that morning, when a bleary-eyed Daphne had dropped off another tray of treats for them to sample, part of the breakfast menu she was putting together for the inn's grand reopening. Daphne hadn't stayed—she was needed at the diner for an early-morning shift, even though she'd worked until closing time the night before—and so Tana and Henry had sat in uncomfortable silence, Henry drumming the finger- tips of his good hand against the tabletop so rapidly that Tana had to continually bite back the urge to beg him to stop.

Not that she could blame him. Tomorrow was a big day.

"Got room for one more up there?" a familiar voice called, and Tana pulled her gaze away from the softly churning ocean to find Edie standing at the end of the inn's cobblestone sidewalk, looking uncharacteristically somber. Without waiting for an invitation, the older woman began making her way toward Tana, her sandals clip-clopping against the stones. When she reached Tana, she dropped into the chair beside her with a sigh and began rocking, their back-and-forth movements in sync with each other and the waves lapping the shore.

"Has Henry said anything about tomorrow?" Edie asked, her voice tight, her eyes on the water.

Tana slid a glance her way, taking in the delicate curve of the woman's cheek and her silver hair that was glowing softly in the moonlight. "Not a word," she murmured, dropping her head against the seat-back and gazing up at the stars. They were innumerable here on the island, where light pollution was scant and the natural world stretched before them in all its beauty. "I think he might be in denial that she's even coming. It's all happening so fast."

Indeed, the past two weeks had flown by, with

Henry becoming more and more withdrawn as the calendar ticked closer to the day of Penny's arrival. He hadn't left the inn at all, other than when Tana accompanied him to his twice-weekly trips to the mainland for physical therapy, but the ferry ride over was even more quiet than usual, leaving Tana to strike up a conversation with Kurt, the friendly captain.

"Do you think he's still in love with her?"

Edie said the words so softly that Tana could scarcely hear her, and when she glanced her way once more, she was shocked to find tears glistening in the older woman's eyes. She let her gaze linger on her for a long moment, but Edie continued watching the ocean, the steady creaking of her rocking chair the only sound between them.

Tana heaved a sigh and ran her fingers through her hair. Finding Penny had consequences not just for Henry, it seemed.

"I don't know," she said honestly. "It's hard for me to get a read on him for anything, let alone this." She laughed hoarsely. "I can't even get a straight answer when I ask him what he'd like for breakfast. The way he hems and haws, you'd think I was asking for his kidney."

"I think he is." Edie's voice was laced with sadness, and Tana saw her fingers tightening on her armrests. "But I suppose that's okay. We all deserve a little happiness in our lives, and Henry has gone too many years without it. Maybe reuniting with Penny will finally bring him the peace he deserves. The peace he's been seeking for all these years."

At those last words, Tana was struck again by how you could spend countless hours, days, *years* with someone, and never truly know them. She had spent each childhood summer under Henry's watchful eye, she and Jax always cracking jokes out of their great-uncle's earshot about his gruff, grouchy exterior. But the more she got to know him now, as an adult, the more she realized that those walls he'd erected around himself were covering up a lifetime of hurt.

Everyone had their own way of dealing with heartbreak. Tana should know that as well as anyone —she had, after all, fled to an island to escape the pain she carried in the aftermath of Derek's betrayal. Henry hadn't run—he'd just hunkered down in the place that brought him comfort, his beloved inn. He'd dedicated his life to his family's inn, and now, in his final years, he deserved to finally have a chance at finding true happiness.

"I'm sorry," she said to Edie, reaching out to squeeze the woman's hand. "I didn't mean for you to get hurt in all of this."

"Oh, honey, this isn't your fault." Edie laughed softly and shook her head. "The day I let myself fall for Henry Turner was the day I opened myself up to a world of hurt. And that's okay—because what's life without a little love in it, even if those feelings aren't reciprocated? That's something I'm only coming to learn now, and I've made my peace with it. What will be, will be."

Then she turned sly eyes Tana's way, the corners of her mouth lifting in a slight smile. "But as for you—I don't think love's quite done with you yet. And when it happens, don't let the opportunity pass you by."

They heard footsteps crunching in the gravel, and both women looked up to find Reed walking through the inn's parking lot, heading their way.

"You know," Edie said, rising from her chair with a mischievous glint in her eye, "I think I may have left the shop door unlocked. I'd better check it before I head off to bed." She stepped off the porch, stopping to kiss her son's cheek before ambling down the sidewalk toward town and out of sight.

Tana sat up straighter as Reed approached her, suddenly nervous. "Hey," he said, gazing up at her from the front yard. "Mind if I join you, or do you want some alone time?"

"Please." Tana gestured to the chair Edie had just

vacated. "Have a seat. I'm just enjoying the view for a while before I head off to bed."

"No better way to relax than by the ocean," Reed murmured, lowering himself into the chair and joining her as she gazed out over the water. Far in the distance, a sea bird dipped in and out of the waves, hunting for its evening meal, and the ferry chugged toward the harbor, kicking up sea spray in its wake.

The minutes ticked by as they sat together in companionable silence, until eventually, Tana tore her eyes from the view and studied Reed's profile, Edie's words playing in her mind. She opened her mouth, intent on saying something—though what that would be, she wasn't entirely sure—but the thought was cut short when Reed took a deep breath and turned to her, his pale eyes gazing directly into hers.

"I have feelings for you."

"Oh," Tana said softly. "I—"

"If it's okay with you," Reed cut in gently, "I'd like to add something to that thought."

He looked at her, and she nodded, gesturing for him to continue. Her stomach was fluttering with nerves as his eyes landed on hers once more. "I think since the minute you stormed into the inn's back-yard and accused me of taking advantage of your uncle"—he chuckled—"I've known that you were special. Since then, since really getting to know you, my feelings have only grown. But you've got a lot going on in your life right now, and I recognize and respect that. If you're not ready, just say the word. If you're never going to be ready, I accept that. But if you are ready…"

He let the rest of the sentence linger in the air between them, along with the promise of something more. Tana took a deep breath herself, then reached over and took his hand. "If you had said this to me before I went to California, my answer might have been different. Not because I don't care about you, but because, like you said, things have been… difficult lately, I guess you could say."

She laughed softly. "But being there only showed me what I was missing here, and I don't just mean the island itself, or the inn, or my uncle, or Edie and Daphne… I mean you, Reed. Above all else, I mean you. And if you'd like to see where this might go, then I'm open to it. With my whole heart, I'm open to it."

And she was. Sometime during these past few weeks, when she closed her eyes at night, Derek's face had faded into the background. A part of her would always love him for the years they'd shared, and for the daughter they'd raised, and another part would always be heartbroken that things played out the way they did. But if her great-uncle's story had taught her anything, it was that she needed to seize what she wanted before it was too late, before she had to endure a lifetime of regret.

"Good." Reed gave her that lopsided grin she loved so much, then released her hand. "Good, good, good." He pressed his palms to his thighs before raising himself off the chair while Tana frowned at him in confusion.

"Where are you going?" she asked, not bothering to conceal the bewilderment in her tone.

By now, Reed had crossed the porch and was taking the steps two at a time. When he reached the bottom, he turned and gave her a playful look, waving his finger toward her sternly. "It's late and I'm off to bed. You should get some sleep too—after all, you have a big day tomorrow." And then, with a wave and a salute, he turned and walked off into the night.

"He just...walked away?" Daphne gave Tana an incredulous look. "Like, he didn't try to kiss you or anything, after he practically declared his love for you?"

181

"Not even a handshake."

Despite yesterday evening's odd turn of events, Tana could barely keep the grin off her face. Even though Uncle Henry had been pacing the inn all night, the thump of his cane on the hardwood floors keeping Tana awake into the early morning hours, she felt refreshed and ready to take on the day.

She and Daphne were currently hunkered down in the inn's kitchen, preparing a platter of sandwiches and cookies for Uncle Henry's reunion with Penny, who was due to arrive in less than an hour. Tana had volunteered to pick her up at the harbor, and a white-faced Henry had readily agreed before retreating to his room, where he'd been all morning, his silence broken only by the intermittent thumping of his cane as, presumably, he paced his room too.

Daphne shook her head in bewilderment. "I don't get it. But I guess I don't get men in general—why else would I have such trouble finding a good one?" Her brow furrowed for a moment, then she shrugged and continued arranging chocolate chip cookies on a serving platter.

"Don't worry, you're not alone," Tana said with a laugh. "Sometimes I think the opposite sex does things to confound us on purpose. You know, to keep life interesting. Take Uncle Henry, for instance

—a few weeks ago, he was desperate for me to help him find Penny. Now, she's arriving in"—Tana checked the time on her phone—"forty *minutes*, and he's barely uttered two words about it." She unrolled a sheet of plastic wrap and tore it off before securing it around the sandwiches and sliding the platter into the refrigerator.

"Are you going to be there?" Daphne asked, leaning against the counter, arms crossed casually as she watched Tana make a pitcher of lemonade. "When they see each other for the first time?" She clasped her hands together, eyes shining with excitement. "How do you think they'll greet each other?"

"I can only imagine what Uncle Henry's going to do." Tana shook her head as she added ice to the pitcher and began stirring the contents with a wooden spoon. "But no, I'm not going to be there—I want to give them their privacy. I'm going to be in the front yard planting some flowers I picked up at the nursery yesterday. I figure that'll keep me busy enough to give me a good distraction."

Daphne groaned. "If it were me, I'd be listening at the door. Heck, I'd have my ear *pressed* against the door! Especially since you went to all that trouble to find her."

Tana shrugged. "I was happy to do it. Uncle Henry was a big part of my life growing up, and even though he can be a little difficult at times, I want what's best for him." She frowned as she recalled the expression of sadness on Edie's face as they spoke last night, but she did her best to shake off the unsettled feeling it gave her. Uncle Henry had made the decision to find Penny, and Tana would support him —she just wished no one else had to get hurt in the process.

She and Daphne finished the preparations for lunch and then spent a few minutes chatting before Tana headed out to the inn's parking lot and slid into the driver's seat of Uncle Henry's golf cart, which she'd be borrowing to pick up Penny. As she drove along the island's winding dirt paths, the untamed dune grass grazed the tires and the wind whipping off the ocean tousled her hair.

When the horizon came into view, Tana could see the ferry chugging into the harbor, and she squinted at the tiny, distant faces of the passengers, trying to make out Penny among them. Then she realized with a laugh that she was searching for the Penny she'd seen in her uncle's old photographs, and not the woman she had become six decades later. Would Uncle Henry even recognize her when they finally met again?

When the ferry shuddered to a halt, bobbing slightly in the gentle waves, Tana watched the passengers disembark, her heart in her throat. It was a beautiful day, and the seating area was packed with both vacationers and islanders who'd had business to attend to on the mainland, but there, among the hustle and bustle as the passengers gathered their bags and headed for the ramp, was a woman sitting alone.

Her shoulder-length silver hair was shining in the sunlight streaming down from the crystalline sky, and she had a coral scarf wrapped around her neck, highlighting her delicate features that had softened slightly with age. When she finally disembarked and crossed the ramp to Tana, her ocean-blue eyes were sparkling with happiness—and just a hint of nerves—as she held out a dainty hand and said, "Hello, you must be Tana. I'm Penny."

Tana shook her hand, then pulled her into a spontaneous hug, blinking back tears as she breathed in the delicate floral perfume Penny wore. "I'm so, *so* glad to meet you," she whispered, releasing Penny from the embrace. Tana retreated a few steps and smiled at her. "There's someone who's been waiting a long time to see you."

CHAPTER 17

*H*enry Turner paced his small room, stopping every so often to steady himself on his cane before resuming his endless circular march. Every time he passed the old wooden roll-top desk that had belonged to his mother, he averted his eyes from the bundle of photographs now lying on its surface. He couldn't look at Penny right now. He couldn't even breathe.

This was a mistake. He should have let sleeping dogs lie. He had been *happy*, for Pete's sake.

He stopped pacing, gripping his cane and catching his breath. Okay, so maybe happy was a stretch. But he had come to terms with the heartbreak of the past many, many years ago, and what good could come of dredging up all those memories again? He wouldn't blame Penny if she had agreed to come to the island merely to give him a swift slap across the face. It was nothing more than he deserved.

I don't love you anymore.

Those words—that filthy lie—had haunted him for more than sixty years. Even now, he sometimes had a hard time believing he had said them. Or better yet, that Penny had believed them herself. He had never made a secret of the fact that she was everything to him.

Which was why he'd had to let her go.

Henry resumed his pacing again, cursing his bad leg for dragging on the floor and slowing him down. He was just about to start another circle around the room when he stopped abruptly, his ears catching the distant sound of tires on gravel, followed a few moments later by two golf cart doors slamming.

She was here.

Henry sank onto the bed, his hands trembling, as the front door opened and closed. A split-second later, Tana called out, "Uncle Henry?"

Taking a deep breath, Henry gazed at his reflection in the mirror, his expression resolute.

Time to face the ghosts of his past, once and for all.

THE FIRST THING Henry noticed about Penny now was the first thing he had noticed about her when they were seven years old. Her eyes, as blue as the ocean, as sparkling as the sun. They were still beautiful, still bursting with intelligence and liveliness and laughter.

And just like that, sixty-four years fell away.

"Henry." Penny stepped forward to greet him. "It's been so long."

He was dimly aware of Tana excusing herself, followed by the distant sound of the front door closing quietly, as Penny pulled him into a long, gentle embrace. He closed his eyes against her familiar scent, immediately carried back to the countless summer evenings they'd spent on the boardwalk, their hands entwined as they gazed out over the darkening water.

He'd missed her. Oh, how he'd missed her.

"Hello, Penny." His voice came out gravelly, as if he hadn't used it in some time, and he quickly cleared his throat. "How are you?"

She smiled. "I can't complain." Then her eyes traveled over to his cane, and a look of concern flashed across her features. "And you?"

"The old ticker's still going, so I can't complain either."

He led her into the inn's parlor, where he was

surprised to see that someone—presumably Tana—had laid out a spread of sandwiches and cookies, along with a pitcher of lemonade and two glasses. He gestured for Penny to help herself, then waited for her to choose a seat in an old armchair before lowering himself onto the couch opposite her.

"Sorry about the mess," he said, waving at the tools and paint cans scattered around the room. Tana had asked the crew to take the day off so he and Penny would have time to talk uninterrupted, and for that, he was grateful. Now that she was here, he had plenty to get off his chest.

The problem was, he had no idea where to start.

Penny, sensing his hesitation, looked around the room with a smile and a shake of her head. "It looks practically the same as it did all those years ago. I have such fond memories of this place, and the island. My parents moved, you know. Not long after…"

Her voice trailed off, and she lowered her gaze to her hands. She studied them for a while, clenched tightly in her lap, before she raised her eyes to his and said, "I've had a good life, Henry. I just want you to know that."

He swallowed hard. "You don't know what it means to me to hear you say that."

"I was angry at you." She cocked her head, staring

at him with those eyes that pierced directly into his soul. "For a long time, I was so, so angry at you." She took a deep breath. "But then, one day—I don't know what it was about that day. I was sitting in a café in the middle of Times Square, drinking a coffee and working on a magazine article and not thinking about you at all, when it dawned on me what had happened. It dawned on me what you had done, and it hit me like a sack of bricks, right here." She pressed her hand over her heart. "You gave me up because you felt like you had to. Not because you wanted to."

Henry's eyes welled up with tears as he remembered that long-ago night when he had made the decision that would forever alter the course of their lives. "What other choice did I have, Penny?" he whispered. "You were ready to soar... and I couldn't be the one to hold you back. I couldn't give you the things that you wanted—and what *I* wanted, above all else, was for you to be happy. Even if it was at the expense of my own happiness."

There was a long pause before Penny dabbed at her eyes and said, "I know that now. And Henry... I thank you, from the bottom of my heart. Because of you, I had a career I loved, and I found a man I loved, and even though he's been gone for many years now, he lives on in the children we had together. Children who were cherished and adored beyond all measure. If not for you, I would never have had those things—because you were right, Henry. I would have stayed, because I loved you. And I still love you. Nothing has changed that—not the years, not the distance, not the circumstances. Nothing."

"Oh, Penny." Henry felt his lungs constricting with emotion, but he fought it back so he could choke out the four words he had longed to say, the four words that would right his wrongs and allow him to forgive himself, finally, for the gut-wrenching decision no teenage boy should have ever had to make. "I love you too. Now and always."

Penny reached across the space separating them and gripped his hand. They remained like that for a long time, holding on as if the other were a lifeline, before she settled back in her chair, crossed one leg over the other, and gave him a smile that still somehow managed to send tingles down his spine. "Now tell me, Henry Turner, what have you been up to for the past sixty-four years?"

TANA GLANCED up from her position kneeling beside the flowerbed, wiping the sweat from her brow before shielding her eyes from the glaring sun. She heard the unmistakable thumping of her uncle's cane before she saw him emerge from the inn, alone. He gazed around the front yard before his eyes landed on hers and he slowly limped forward, descending the porch steps with difficulty before making his way across the dewy grass toward her.

He came to a halt in front of her, his shadow looming over her and the flowers she had spent the last hour planting, glancing every so often at the inn's picture window and wondering what was going on inside. Where was Penny, anyway?

"I just wanted to say thank you." Henry's normally gruff tone was replaced with a softer one, and she was surprised to see the corners of his eyes crinkling with the hint of a smile. "Because of you, life can move on."

"I'm so glad." Tana rose to her feet, brushing dirt off her knees before taking a tentative step forward and pulling the old man into a hug. He hesitated for a few seconds and then returned the embrace, his good arm tightening around her waist before he stepped back and patted her clumsily on the arm.

"You're a good kid."

Tana laughed, then glanced at the inn before giving Henry a questioning look. "Penny is…?"

"Inside," Henry said. "We're going to enjoy a nice lunch together in a few minutes before we take a little tour of the island, visit some of our old haunts. The ones that are still standing, that is."

"So what now?" Tana asked the question that had been burning a hole in her mind. "What happens next?"

"Now," Henry said, taking a deep breath, "I'm going to go ask my sweetheart out on a date. It's been a long time coming." Then he turned and began limping down the sidewalk toward town.

"Wait!" Tana called after him, her confused glance going to the inn, where Penny was waiting, back to Henry as he stopped and faced her. "Where are you going?"

Henry smiled. "I just told you."

And then he turned around once more and continued walking away from the inn.

This time, he was whistling.

CHAPTER 18

*E*die sat at her desk, one hand resting beneath her chin, the other drumming the wooden surface absentmindedly. It had been a particularly slow day at the shop, and time seemed like it was moving at a crawl, just when she wanted nothing more than for it to speed up so she could put this awful day behind her once and for all.

Her eyes drifted to the window, where she could see the inn's rooftop just visible through the trees, before she averted her gaze and looked around the store, desperate for something to do. She could straighten the antique furniture for the tenth time, or sweep a dust rag over the impeccably clean shelves, or mop the streak-free floors. She could do just about anything but torture herself by imagining what was going on inside that inn at this very moment.

Reed, bless his heart, had stopped by a few times already, always with an excuse that he needed to drop off a package, or see if she wanted him to grab lunch, or—most laughably—if he could borrow a few bucks to put gas in his golf cart. The last time her son had asked her for cash, he was ten years old —Reed was as self-sufficient as they came, a hard worker with a desire for independence that ran through his veins like blood.

But she was comforted by his presence all the same.

Edie straightened in her chair as a pair of women strolled past the window, looking at the selection of old rotary phones on display—for reasons Edie couldn't fathom, they were becoming a hot-ticket item, even though to her they were just regular old phones she'd used her entire life. The women waved when they caught her watching them, then lingered on the sidewalk for a few moments before moving on, leaving Edie to slump back down again and heave a long sigh.

The minutes ticked by endlessly as Edie stared at the clock. Finally, when she could stand it no longer, she got up and strode into the storage area at the back of the shop, determined to comb through some of the new inventory so she could move it to the sales floor as soon as possible. She had just fetched her notebook and label maker when the bell above the front door chimed.

Dropping her things onto the nearest table, Edie straightened her blouse—she had chosen a white one with big coral flowers today, her favorite, in an attempt to brighten her mood—and headed into the shop's main area.

"Hello," she called as she stepped through the door. "Welcome to Antiques on the—"

"Am I?" Henry said, his green eyes latching onto hers. "Welcome, that is." He was standing by the front desk, leaning heavily on his cane.

And he was alone.

"I don't know what you're talking about, you old kook." Edie brushed past him, then turned and crossed her arms over her chest. "Where's your girlfriend?"

Henry adjusted his stance, wincing slightly, and Edie was overcome with the urge to help him. Henry Turner was as independent as they came, but she was a born nurturer, and she couldn't stand to see anyone in discomfort.

"Penny's back at the inn, waiting for me," Henry said as Edie pulled out the chair behind the desk and began pushing it toward him. She froze momentarily at his words, but then forced herself to keep a neutral expression as she delivered the chair to him.

"Oh. That's nice."

"Yes." Those green eyes were still piercing hers, leaving her feeling distinctly uncomfortable. "We're going to enjoy the day together, and then Penny's leaving on the evening ferry. I expect this will be the last time I'll see her." He was still standing, ignoring the chair altogether, his attention entirely focused on Edie's face.

She gave him a blank look. "Why? The reunion didn't go well?"

"It went perfectly." Henry took a deep breath. "The questions that have been tormenting me for more than six decades have been answered, and I can finally, finally move on with my life."

Edie blinked at him. Why was she having such a hard time following the thread of this conversation? She opened her mouth to say something, but Henry cut her off, shuffling his cane to the side and reaching forward to grasp her hand.

For goodness' sake, Edie thought, glaring at him. Why couldn't that old bag of bones look away for a moment and give her some *space*?

"Edie." Henry chuckled. "Can't you see it's you that I love? It's been that way for, oh, going on twenty years now, I think." When Edie mouthed wordlessly at him, he said, "I couldn't fully move on —I couldn't *allow* myself to move on—until I knew that Penny was happy. And today, I learned that she was. She had a beautiful life. She actually *thanked* me, Edie. She thanked me."

His voice caught, and he squeezed his eyes shut, pinching the bridge of his nose for a long moment before opening them again and meeting her gaze once more.

This time, she didn't look away.

"So I came here," Henry said, inhaling deeply, as if steeling himself for something, "to ask you, Edie Dawes, if you would do an old man the distinct pleasure of allowing him to take you out for dinner tomorrow night?"

Edie narrowed her eyes at Henry for several long moments, considering him. Finally, she said simply, "No."

Henry looked thrown. "No?" he repeated.

"No," Edie said, more firmly this time. "I've waited long enough. You can take me out for lunch instead."

Henry blinked at her, and then all of a sudden he threw his head back, his laughter ringing through the shop.

Before long, Edie joined in.

TANA SAT on her favorite wicker rocking chair with a glass of lemonade by her side and sighed happily. This day had been a long time coming, and to call it a success would be an understatement. Earlier, she'd stepped into the inn to make herself a quick sandwich and heard Henry and Penny giggling like a couple of teenagers in the parlor as they recounted their childhoods on the island and shared memories of their old friends.

Then they had left for a tour of their favorite spots, and now Uncle Henry was accompanying Penny on the last ferry over to the mainland. Tana was worried his mobility issues would make traveling by himself on the ferry for the return trip perilous, but Kurt, the captain, had promised Tana he would keep a watchful eye on her uncle.

And now, finally, she could relax.

Tana raised the glass of lemonade to her lips and was preparing to take her first sip when her phone rang, cutting through the silence like a knife and almost making her jump out of her skin. Fearing that something had happened to Uncle Henry after all, she immediately grabbed it and checked the caller ID. When she saw Daphne's name, she considered letting it go to voicemail—the Penny and Henry gossip could wait until morning—but she answered at the last second and was immediately glad she did.

"Tana?" Daphne's voice sounded slightly panicked, which immediately set the alarm bells blaring.

Tana shot up in her chair, her lemonade swishing over the top of the glass. "Daphne? What's the matter?"

"Nothing. Ugh." Tana could practically hear Daphne wincing through the phone. "I decided to go for a walk on the beach after work, and I stepped in a hole some kids had dug and now I think I've sprained my ankle. Can you pick me up? Sorry to be a pain… I'm sure you're trying to take the night off."

"Don't worry about that for a second. I'm on my way. See you in a few." Tana was already bounding down the porch steps toward the golf cart. She turned the key in the ignition, backed out of the inn's gravel lot, and began the quick drive down the winding dirt path that led to the sand. When she arrived, she parked in the small lot, slid the keys in her pocket, and jogged onto the sand, scanning the moonlit beach for Daphne.

"Over here," someone called, and Tana swung around to see Reed at the water's edge, holding a bouquet of wildflowers and standing beside a table set for two. A white tablecloth billowed softly in the ocean breeze, and a bottle of champagne and two crystal flutes glittering in the moonlight were placed in the middle of the table, along with two plates piled high with a sumptuous-looking dinner, and Daphne's chocolate mousse pie for dessert.

"What's all this?" Tana asked, stepping over to Reed, kicking up sand as she walked. Her heart was in her throat as she stopped in front of him and he gazed down at her for a long moment, his pale eyes soft as they met hers. He pressed the bouquet into her arms.

"I'm sorry I left things hanging between us last night. As soon as you said you wanted to give us a try, I knew I had to plan something special… but I also knew I needed to wait until after Henry and Penny had their reunion and you could relax and enjoy the evening. So…" He gestured toward the table. "For you. And me. And us."

Then he pulled out her chair and waited for her to sit before settling into the chair opposite her. He bent down and fiddled with something beneath the table, and a moment later, soft musical notes drifted toward Tana's ears on the saltwater breeze.

"I'm also sorry for making you come here under false pretenses," he said, his eyes twinkling with laughter as he uncorked the champagne and began filling her glass. "But I couldn't figure out a way to get you down here without ruining the surprise, and Daphne had this great idea, and, well, you know the rest..."

"It's lovely," Tana said, smiling softly at Reed as he passed her the glass. She began raising it to her lips, then stopped, cocking her head at him. "We should have a toast."

"We should," Reed agreed, raising his own glass. He held it out to her, his eyes on hers. Then he took a deep breath and began, "I know neither of us knows where this is going, but..." He smiled. "I can't wait to find out." He kept his gaze on her as they both sipped their drinks, and when they had finished, he set down his glass and held out his hand.

"Before we enjoy our main course, brought to you by the delicious Sal's Diner"—he grinned at her, causing her stomach to flip-flop again—"may I have this dance?" He rose from his seat and took her hand, and together they walked toward the water's edge, kicking off their shoes and allowing their bare feet to sink into the pillowy sand.

Then, as the moonlight danced around them and the stars glittered in an endless sky, Tana rested her head on Reed's chest, and they danced.

EPILOGUE

"Wait for me," Jax shouted, hurrying down the weathered ramp just as the ferry churned to life. The captain turned and waved to him, signaling that he had heard him, and Jax hurried onboard, dragging his suitcase behind him, and sighed with relief as he dropped into a chair.

The sky had darkened almost to black, and Jax was grateful that he had managed to make it to town in time to catch the last ferry of the night. Grateful also that he was alone, with nothing but his thoughts to keep him company; that, and the rhythmic sound of the waves lapping against the ferry as they pulled away from the harbor and began the brief journey to the island.

Wait. Not alone.

Jax caught sight of an elderly man sitting on the far side of the ferry opposite him, one hand clenched around the top of his cane as he gazed out over the water. Jax studied him for a moment; the darkness was thick, and he was having a hard time determining if he knew the man. Probably—everyone on the island knew everyone else, and Jax had spent many summers exploring its windswept shores and getting to know the townspeople. But many years had passed since then, and even if he did know the man, it was a safe bet that he wouldn't recognize Jax.

Which was how he preferred it right now. What Jax needed more than anything was a break. And that included a break from awkward conversations with a person he hadn't seen in twenty-five years.

The man caught Jax watching him, and Jax gave him a swift nod before settling back into his seat and closing his eyes. The last few days—heck, the last few *years*—had left him exhausted, and he wanted nothing more than to drift off to—

Thump. Thump. Thump.

Jax shot up to find the man standing in front of him, leaning heavily on his cane, his eyes wide with shock.

"Jax?" the old man said in disbelief, in a voice that was unmistakably familiar. "What are *you* doing here?"

THANK you for reading **The Gilded Days**, the second book in the Dolphin Bay series. Book three, **The Magic Hour**, will be available soon, so be sure to sign up for my email list to be the first to know about release day. I'll never share your information with anyone.

To stay connected, check out my Facebook page, send me an email at miakentromance@gmail.com, or visit my website at www.miakent.com. I love to hear from my readers!

And to help indie authors like me continue bringing you the stories you love, please consider leaving a review of this book on the retailer of your choice.

Thank you so much for your support!

Love,

Mia

MIA KENT IS the author of clean, contemporary women's fiction and small-town romance. She writes heartfelt stories about love, friendship, happily ever after, and the importance of staying true to yourself.

She's been married for over a decade to her high school sweetheart, and when she isn't working on her next book, she's chasing around a toddler, crawling after an infant, and hiding from an eighty-pound tornado of dog love. Frankly, it's a wonder she writes at all.

To learn more about Mia's books, to sign up for her email list, or to send her a message, visit her website at www.miakent.com.

Printed in Great Britain
by Amazon